Wind Chimes

Teresa Adele Bettino

Wind Chimes by Teresa Adele Bettino

ISBN 13: 978-0-9742842-4-8

Michael Paust

Michael Paust grew up in Webster, NY, a small town in upstate, NY. After attaining an MBA in marketing and international business, he landed in Athens, Greece for his first job as a management consultant. Next he was off to South Africa where he spent nearly a year working as a consultant during the week and photographing animals and landscapes on the weekend. Michael later worked for extended periods of time in The Philippines, South Korea, Prague, Saudi Arabia, and finally Ireland where he spent considerable time photographing the country's Western coast. During his travel, he developed a passion for and perfected his style of photography. He began to photograph the people, the landscapes, and the coastlines of the places where he lived and worked. After 2000, he made many trips to Mexico, the Dominican Republic, and the Caribbean where he continued to photograph people, and coastal areas. It wasn't until the summer of 2005 when he met his wife Melissa he began photographing the people and coastline of Long Beach Island, NJ. Michael incorporates a variety of lighting and exposure techniques into his work. He prefers candid style shooting because it allows him to more effectively capture the true personalities of his subjects. Outside of photography, Michael has a successful career as a Corporate Vice President for a New York based professional services firm that operates in 42 countries.

Email: *mike@michaelpaust.com*

Website: *www.michaelpaust.com*

Not westward,
But
Eastward seek the
Coming of light

(Dakota)

Dedication

For my better half, I love you.
You keep me centered.

And to Judy Berger, my partner in crime.

Acknowledgements

Mariner, Kirk: *Off 13 The Eastern Shore of Virginia Guidebook*, Miona Publications New Church, Virginia 23415, 2002.

Zona, Guy A.: *The Soul Would Have No Rainbow if the Eyes Had No Tears and Other Native American Proverbs,* Simon and Schuster, 1994.

Maps: www.chincoteague.com and Virginia Film Office-Virginia is for Lovers

Special thanks to Nancy Wilmink and Christopher Green for their technical assistance.

Chincoteague Island, Virginia

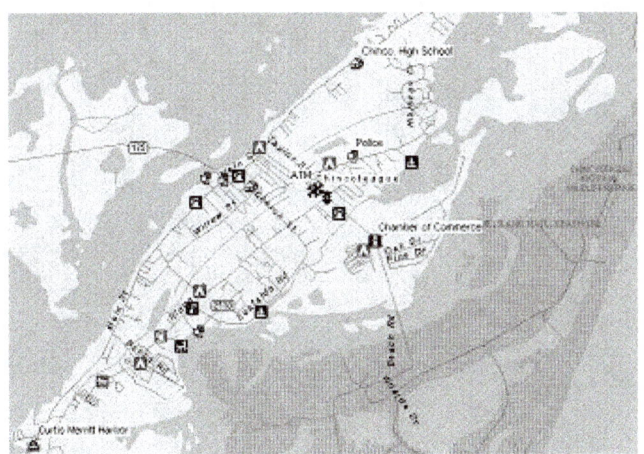

Virginia Eastern Shore

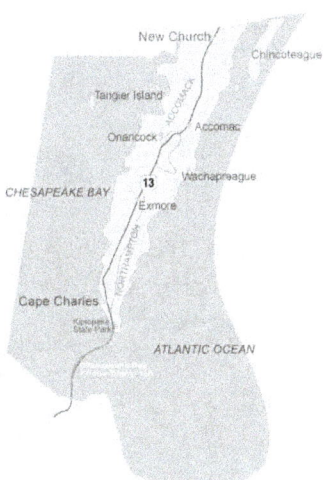

New Church

Chincoteague

Tangier Island

ACCOMAC

Onancock

Accomac

Wachapreague

13

CHESAPEAKE BAY

Exmore

NORTHAMPTON

Cape Charles

Kiptopeke
State Park

ATLANTIC OCEAN

Wind Chimes

Teresa Adele Bettino

1

"Monday, Monday, can't trust that day," was ringing in my ears as I awoke. The Mamas and the Papas was something that I listened to during childhood, as my mother was a "child of the sixties."

It wasn't hot, foggy, buggy or rainy. It was Monday. What's the other song about Monday by Karen Carpenter, "Rainy days and Mondays, always get me down" or something similar? My mom used to hum it along with the Mamas and the Papas waking me up for school. To this day, I dread that Monday morning nervous stomach.

The alarm goes off. I don't want to get out of bed and face another day. My brain is functioning but my legs don't want to move. I groan and stretch simultaneously and decide that it is time to move. I give a good grunt from the bottom of my belly as I toss the layers of covers off of me. My feet hit the carpeted floor.

Sophie, my tabby feline, is stretched across the carpet. She's directly in front of the television. I need to use the bathroom and take a quick shower. As I walk past Sophie, my big toe gets attached to her back leg and I stumble, falling into the TV. The TV proceeds to fall off its stand and crashes onto the floor scaring Sophie, who takes off under my grandmother's old iron bed.

So starts my workweek. I live in Chincoteague, Virginia, a barrier island, located on the Eastern Shore and my name is Francie Batista. I work for, or is it; I am employed by the Department of Social Services. I'm a transplant to this area having been raised in Richmond.

After my shower, I feed Sophie some dry food, and my mind is racing. Since it's Monday I have lots to do, like going out on home visits to check on children and adults. This morning I shower and dress quickly, so I have time to check e-mails. I recently had my hair cut, and I run my fingers through my new short hair. I decided that it was time to go back to basics, a pixie hairstyle. It's perfect. No fuss, just stick my head under the faucet and in one minute I have my curly hair under control. With a little gel, it doesn't curl as much.

Living on an island affords me the luxury of not having to fill my gas tank every few days. I don't drive to work, I ride my bike and like the mailman, I ride in rain, gales of wind, sleet and snow. Yes, it does snow at the beach and what the heck; it keeps me in shape. My office is in the back portion of a small peeling wooden building between Sundial Book Store, on the corner of Main Street and the charming Chincoteague Library, located in front of a small park. My small cramped office is situated off of the building's kitchen and has a beautiful view of the park and the Chincoteague Bay. What else could I ask for at age twenty-four?

Piles of papers are on the floor, desk and file drawers, which are so filled that they stay opened. That describes my office. I inherited this mess. It's generational. The worker before me retired. Thirty years, of "wedded bliss" is how April Lakefield described her journey as a social worker. I've often wondered if she was facetious or honest. I'm basically on my own out here. I do check in with my supervisor, Sally-Sue Moon once in awhile, when I have a question. When I can't find my supervisor, which is often, I contact her supervisor, Juney Bea Karring.

I investigate child abuse and adult abuse reports. I sometimes work with an investigator from the sheriff's department named Jodi Burgess. She's a newfound friend. Jodi's about thirty-five and loves the single life along with new blings and adventures. Like me, she came here after graduation from Virginia

Commonwealth University also known as VCU, and decided to live at the beach. "Life's a beach" and for Jodi and me, we love the slower pace, sand, sea, and fresh fish.

As I enter my office, I sneeze, and quickly reach for tissues. The box is empty. A crying client visited with me on Friday. Diane Tate either calls daily or visits me at least once per week to discuss her life. Very little has been resolved. Her cheating worthless husband left her barefoot and pregnant. Diane cried through a whole tissue box as I tried to console her. I'm not very good at consoling somebody who has done it to themselves, so to speak. Another saying, "You made your bed, now lie in it." I wonder if anybody has made a country song from that short sentence, which says it all. I know that I sound heartless, but really I'm a compassionate person or else I wouldn't be in the human service field, now would I? It's Diane's fifth child, and she's twenty-nine years old. Try using some birth control!

I spot a half roll of toilet paper, sitting on the radiator in the bathroom and grab for it.

The phone rings as I blow my nose. I catch the phone on the second ring.

"Hello, partner in crime," Jodi Burgess says with a giggle.

"What's up?" I stutter and continue to blow my nose.

"You sound like you have a cold."

"Nope, it's called dust, mold and bay."

"We just got a call about a dead body that showed itself at Muddy Creek, off of Route 683."

"Jodi, how many times have I told you that I only investigate the living?"

"I know, but I think we need to work this together, as this guy is about seventy. I think he could be an elderly resident that may have wandered out of the adult home in Guilford.

"You mean, Friendship Place?"

"Yeah, I can pick you up in about forty-five minutes."

"You can't be serious," I reply reaching to my right bottom desk drawer for some chocolate candies.

"I'll treat you to some coffee at Fast Mart."

"How about treating me to some real coffee at Main Street Shop Coffeehouse? Let me call my supervisor and let her know what's happened in case this makes Breaking News."

I speed-dial my supervisor, Sally-Sue Moon, who reminds me of a retired race horse named Sally that I once exercised at the Meadow Farm, in Caroline County, a little north of Richmond. Both have sway-backs, sagging bellies and collectively are horse's asses to be around.

Although Sally-Sue is from Lexington, Virginia, she has a drawl from somewhere that I

21

haven't quite figured out. Her mom named her after a distant relative who ran away from home and joined a band of gypsies. This is what my mom has told me about Sally-Sue's past, as mom, Juney Bea and Sally-Sue went to Virginia Tech together, and all majored in social work. Sally-Sue's a global thinker. You can see it in her stars for eyes, ears for planets and the galaxy on her hips as she ingests Milky Way bars by the dozen when stressed.

On the other hand, I'm a direct communicator, which makes it unbearable for me to be in the same room with Sally-Sue, let alone work with her on projects. I inevitably end up doing all the paperwork, as paperwork isn't Sally-Sue's forte.

Sally-Sue's secretary, Erma Watson, is just short of a military drill sergeant. She served in Iraq and tries hard to keep everything needing retention and attention in her brain to transfer to the brain of Sally-Sue. This transfer doesn't usually work.

"Hi Erma, is Sally-Sue at work yet?"

"No. She just called from the McDonald's near Cape Charles. She had ordered her breakfast, paid and drove off without the order. She remembered about three miles up Route 13, made a U-turn in the middle of four lanes of traffic. The sheriff's deputy has stopped her and is giving her a ticket as we speak."

"Well, I'm sorry to hear that," I reply, reaching for my second round of candy. I take a swig of an old opened bottled of water left on my desk from Friday and almost spit it out.

"Let her know that I'm going out in the field with Investigator Burgess. A body of an elderly man has been found at Muddy Creek. Jodi thinks that the man is from the nearby adult home in Guilford," I say as I smile, thinking of Sally-Sue getting a ticket.

"I'll have my cell phone on if Sally-Sue wants to talk. Isn't this about her fifth ticket in the past three months? I bet she will need to attend driving school so that her insurance doesn't go up."

"Francie, this is the third ticket in the past month. I think they might pull her license. I'll let Sally-Sue know where you are when she gets here. I'll call if you are needed."

2

I flip my cell phone off and hear a distant horn. It's Jodi sitting in the back parking lot waiting to take me to Friendship Place. I grab my purse and looked out of the window. One of the stray cats, along with a flock of waddling ducks is waiting for a hand-out. I hastily grab some cat food from the kitchen cabinet and leave the office through the side kitchen door. As I feed the stray I notice three more cats waiting for me to leave. I scoot through a small alley near the library and Sundial Book Store and into Jodi's car. The ducks have congregated and are quacking. They enjoy dry cat food, as does every seagull in a two-mile radius. There's major commotion outside of the bookstore where every living animal, it appears, has arrived. Tourists walking around are covering their heads, looking down and running into Sundial Book Store.

"So give me the scoop on this dead man's body." I request, getting into Jodi's car.

24

"He's been dead for about three days. Shot in the head at close range with a 40-Glock handgun."

"Isn't that the type of gun that you carry?"

"Yup. Has anyone been reported missing from Friendship Place?"

"Well, I've been on-call and I haven't received a call from the State Hotline."

"Francie, let's go for coffee and swing by Friendship Place. The body has been removed from Muddy Creek and is on its way to the coroner's office. There's also something really strange about this man's death. Don't repeat this; just keep it to your self."

"OK. Now what? *I hope this has nothing to do with adult protective services. I don't have the time to complete a mass investigation at an adult home.* What's strange?"

"When he was found face down, bloated and partially submerged in creek water, his hands were holding a wind chime."

"What!"

"Between his hands, the dead man was holding a wind chime. And get this; the wind chime is of a horse."

"You can't be serious?" I reply as I get out of Jodi's car and head into Main Street Shop Coffeehouse.

Once inside I stand there in a daze thinking of my horse, Trooper, boarded on the mainland.

25

I am wondering what the meaning is with a horse wind chime and this dead old man.

I order mocha and add whipped cream to make me feel better. I try not to be an emotional eater, but oh well; I'll work it off at the gym tonight. Jodi orders a large black coffee to go, and directs her eyes to the door giving me her "it's time to leave" signal. I try to make conversation, but I'm anxious. I change the subject to one of Jodi's favorites, Sally-Sue Moon.

"Jodi, you won't believe what a mess Sally-Sue's in. She's gotten another traffic ticket."

"What did she do now?"

"She made a U-turn on Route 13 as she forgot to pick up her McDonald's order."

"I think this time she's going to either lose her license or be ordered to go to driving school."

I take a sip of mocha and smile. Deep in thought we slow down to let the waddling ducks cross the street with their ducklings. This is another reason why I love living here. No place on Earth do you spend an enormous amount of time waiting for ducks to cross the street.

Once the ducks have crossed, Jodi moves along Main Street. We cross the bridge and view the new bridge in the making.

"I'll really miss this old bridge when we can't travel on it." Jodi says as she drinks her black coffee.

26

"I know. It's a shame that city council voted to spend millions more on a modern bridge, when they could have fixed the old bridge and kept the island looking old-world. But since we're stuck with this multi-million modern bridge, tourists should be able to walk across the old bridge to the mainland."

"Progress." We say in unison.

As we cross the bridge on our way to Guilford to interview the proprietor of Friendship Place, Jodi and I talk about work. I'm the one complaining about work, not Jodi who's getting ready to go on a well-deserved vacation. She's all packed and ready to leave for an all-inclusive week in Key West with one of her girlfriends from college.

I also complain about our director, Juney Bea Karring. She has the reputation of being constricted and is a known witch hunter. At a recent staff meeting Juney Bea described some of us who don't have the best style of clothes and body shapes as "clients waiting in line for welfare."

"Don't tell me that she's still on that jag. Wasn't she lathered last summer about thong sandals?

"Yep, yep. I call her small following the KKK-fashion police. Kathy, Katelyn and Kitty, walk the halls in search of non-compliance. One female staffer, Megan Buxom, who works on

WIND CHIMES Teresa Adele Bettino

broken down computers and is bent over all day,
came to work wearing jeans and a T-shirt on
dress-down day. Of course any shirt that Megan
wears is tight due to her set of knockers. The
worker was told to leave work and directed not
to show her hulking great bosom again. She now
wears maternity tops."

"You can't be serious."

I nod yes, sipping my coffee. "Now, take the
women with big butts. They wear these skirts to
"dress for success" as Juney Bea calls it and
when you walk behind them their skirts are up
their butts however; below the knee in front with
a full moon view in the back!"

While I take another sip of coffee, I envision
walking behind Mona Leonard. Her hips sway
and skirt swings showing layers of buckling fat
over the top of her knees. Juney Bea's concern
is for a professional image; that we don't look
like clients and that we don't wear thong sandals
and spaghetti straps tops. It's the skirts that she
needs to look at.

"Oh well, Juney Bea enjoys her Alpha status.
Then place flighty Sally-Sue next in line and
what a screwed up bunch you have working for
social services." Jodi says as she sips her coffee,
and decides to check-in letting dispatch know her
location.

"You got that right. But then again the
sheriff's department is full of macho-men with

28

testosterone pumping through their groins. Thank God I don't need to be around Sally-Sue and Juney Bea much, as I like macho-men, especially those with high doses of testosterone."

Elizabeth Allen is awakened by the sound of a gun going off in the distance. Bang! The sound startled her Corgi, Princess. Princess began barking and growling. She spun around on the bed, causing the sheets to come off of Elizabeth's shoulders. Elizabeth hates to feel air on her shoulders. She immediately stirs, stretching each leg like walking up a staircase. In her mind, Elizabeth thinks that a car has backfired in the neighborhood. Although the houses are separated by ten acres, a car backfiring would be noticed along this quiet spot of Chincoteague Channel. Watts Estates has several horse farms and Elizabeth owns the last farm on the left. She trains and boards horses. Currently, Elizabeth has four horses boarding and owns two. Her newest addition to her growing family is a two-year-old Chincoteague pony purchased from the auction this past July.

Princess continues to act up and Elizabeth begins to feel concerned as the dog is behaving strangely. Princess is standing on the bed and looking out of the bedroom window. This window faces east, where the horse pastures are

29

located.   The   pastures   face   the   channel.
Elizabeth chose this small bedroom for its view.
It fits her personality, cozy, with an antique
single bed, a white peeling wicker rocker and
one bureau with family photos of her parents and
grandfather, Albert.   Numerous horse and beach
pictures outline the walls.

Having lived in Chincoteague during her
childhood, she moved to the mainland after
inheriting some money from her grandfather.
Her dream has always been to train, sell and own
horses. Both of Elizabeth's parents died in an
airplane crash when she was six. Her grandpa,
Albert Mathews raised her alone as Elizabeth's
grandmother, Mabel died six months prior to her
parents.   Albert and Elizabeth mourned the
deaths of her parents and Mabel. This loss of her
parents and grandmother was almost too much to
bear for Elizabeth.   For Albert his losses were
too much to accept. Acceptance was difficult for
young Elizabeth too.   She had just started
kindergarten when her parents died and was not
able to concentrate. Elizabeth spent most of the
day in class, day dreaming, looking out of the
classroom window watching the wind blow
leaves on trees. Elizabeth, as an only child, was
doted on by her parents especially her father, as
she was "daddy's girl."   Without her parents and
grandmother, she was lost, numb feeling and
morose.

30

Grandpa Albert and Elizabeth were shattered. They needed to love and to be loved. Elizabeth was Albert's reason to live. Unfortunately for Elizabeth having her grandfather twelve years was too short as Albert suffered a massive stroke, just after Elizabeth graduated from Chincoteague High School. With monies from her grandpa's life insurance policy and the sale of Grandpa Albert's house, Elizabeth decided to move away from the island. She purchased this ten-acre plot so that she could surround herself with animals. The emptiness without Grandpa Albert cut through her heart. She didn't want to live her life feeling aloneness, such a painful feeling. Her horses, cats and dog are her family, her security, giving her a sense of direction and purpose.

Elizabeth loves mucking stalls, lunging and training horses, and boarding horses to make ends meet. Money doesn't mean a lot. As long as she can pay her bills she's happy.

Once the land was purchased, Elizabeth hired her boyfriend, James Parker, who owns a small family business on the island called Parker's Odd Jobs. She purchased a modular, green house over the Internet and once delivered, James fine-tuned it. It's just perfect for Elizabeth, Princess, and her indoor cat Harry. At age, eighteen she doesn't need much.

With Princess' continual barking, Elizabeth quickly removes herself from bed. She's already been up and about once today, as she fed her horses at six this morning. Her routine is simple; feed horses, go back to bed, read the newspaper while drinking coffee and listening to the Today Show. Later, she will muck stalls, groom horses and train.

As Princess continues to bark, Elizabeth peers out of the bedroom window. She sees a figure in the middle of the pasture on the ground.

"Oh my God," she screams throwing the newspaper onto the floor, and knocking over her coffee as she tosses a sweat shirt on and shoves her feet quickly into her mucking boots. Running down the stairs two at a time she runs outside with Princess at her heels.

Elizabeth climbs the horse fence, jumps to the ground and twists her ankle. She quickly recovers and continues to run, limping. She runs frantically to Star. Elizabeth stares in disbelief. Star, a Quarter Horse owned by her childhood friend, Maryellen Holmes has been shot in the head.

Elizabeth turns away from the view of Star. She bends over and vomits her morning coffee. She runs, arms flailing. Screeching, Elizabeth runs full speed to her neighbor, Bart Connors. Princess remains at the heels of Elizabeth and can be heard in the distance yelping. Elizabeth climbs Bart Connors' horse fence and continues to run. She sees Bart outside of his barn.

Bart Connors hears all the commotion as he's outside feeding his horses. Elizabeth's hysterical. Bart checks his watch, Monday, 9:05 AM.

3

Jodi and I continue to gossip as we travel to Guilford. We were thinking of looking around Muddy Creek, but it's a crime scene and I don't really want to be a part of looking around where a dead man was. We therefore travel straight to Friendship Place. Friendship Place is located in Guilford, a virtual ghost town. There hasn't been much action in Guilford for hundreds of years. It was first founded by a bunch of Quakers in about 1683.

The adult home is located near an old brick historic farmhouse called Mason House. The house is located in a cotton field and the bricks have been dated to the early 1700's. Friendship Place has about ten residents and it's been newly renovated. The facility sits about one-half mile away in an adjoining field. The field, this time of year, is filled with cotton, just ready for picking.

I notice as we drive into the parking area that the cotton is glistening with morning dew. Maybe this is a good sign seeing the radiance of cotton, on this sunny Monday morning. Hopefully, nobody's going to be missing.

There is twenty-four hour supervision provided to residents to assist with their activities of daily living, such as; bathing, dressing and medication administration. It's licensed by the Department of Social Services and the times that I have come unannounced to the home, everything has been in order.

Jodi parks the car and we get out. We surprise staff with this early visit. The residents are eating pancakes with a slab of bacon. The smell of fresh coffee brewing mixed with bacon is inviting.

"Has Ms. Bannister arrived yet?"

"No, she has a doctor's appointment this morning. Is there anything I can do to help you?"

"Yes, I'm Francie Batista, from social services and I'm here to complete a head count of your residents. Are you new, as I don't seem to have met you?"

"No, I usually work midnights, but switched shifts with Allison. My name is Nancy Jordan."

"Well, Nancy, I received a call from Investigator Jodi Burgess. I'm sorry, I don't know if you know each other."

Jodi smiles and extends her right hand for a good handshake and says, "I think that this is the first time that we've met, Nancy. I contacted

Francie early this morning as a body of an elderly gentleman has been found in Muddy Creek."

"Oh, my goodness! That's horrible. We aren't missing anyone as I completed roll call this morning and everybody's accounted for. Some of the residents are still eating breakfast."

"Well, I need to see a roster of residents and then I need to complete a head count so that I can make sure that this dead man isn't from here."

As Nancy ran around the facility with me beside her, Jodi sat and watched Good Morning America with two residents, Benny and Jerry.

Nancy and I doubled checked and triple checked our head count. No one is unaccounted for.

Ida, a resident that I placed two weeks ago spots me and eagerly rushes over to me. I wince, thinking, *Oh shit, I placed her here and now I still have to see her.* I force a smile and give her a big hug. Mistake number one, I ask how she's doing. This I find to be a rather large error on my part as it opens a huge can of worms.

"Why did you put me here? I was doing fine on my own. They won't let me stand in the shower for more than twenty minutes. I still have germs on me."

Nancy moves closer to me as there's strength in numbers. She places her hand on Ida's shoulder trying to redirect.   We attempt to change the subject. But Ida persists.

I'm thinking this conversation isn't going anywhere.   You have obsessive-compulsive disorder and were going through ten bars of Ivory per day, not taking your medications and calling the sheriff's department inviting them over to go skinny dipping in Tom's Cove with you. You're basically nuts!

Being the compassionate person that I am, I try reframing.

"Ida, I believe that once you get used to living here you will feel better. You can make some friends and be involved with activities. I have to go now, but the next time I come I will spend some time with you. Why don't you come with Nancy and me to the TV room and watch some TV?"

Ida grunts and walks away.

As I proceed down the hallway, making a left onto another corridor, Nancy and I find Jimmy Nelson standing in the hallway saluting. Jimmy is a veteran from World War II.   I recently placed him at Friendship Place due to his self-neglect.   He is in the beginning stage of Alzheimer's. We stop and salute. He smiles and leaves merrily happy.

Once he's down the hallway, Nancy and I are feeling relieved. We proceed to enter the TV

37

room and in the distance can hear Jodi giggling her girlish chuckle with two residents.

She's obviously having a good time as I see a bunch of nickels in front of her. Good Morning America is still serving as background noise and it's apparent that Jodi has taken everybody's money. A resident named Benny appears captivated by Jodi's friendly presence.

Benny grabs Jodi's hand and kisses it as Nancy and I walk up to her.

Smiling Jodi points to Benny with her free hand and laughs.

"You know that you shouldn't do that to me, Benny, as I'm an officer of the law. I'm going to stop our card game as Francie has returned. I'll divide my winnings between Jerry and you. I've enjoyed our card game and the next time I come to Guilford, if I have some time, we'll play poker."

Both men smile and reach for the cash.

I inform Jodi that the dead man isn't from here.

Leaving Friendship Place, heading back to Chincoteague, I notice that clouds have formed and feel that the air has shifted. It's coming from the ocean. The sun is no longer present. A gust of wind carries litter to the steps of Friendship Place. A chill runs up and down my spine as I step over litter and open the passenger door to Jodi's car. My Italian grandmother would have

38

said that, "Somebody's just walked over my grave."

Driving back to Chincoteague, I'm deep in thought. I'm hopeful that the only other worker in this satellite office has shown up for work. After all it is Monday. The main Department of Social Services building is located in Accomack County, about a thirty-minute drive South on Route 13. Although working in a satellite office is nice, it can be brutal when you're the only one there. Wanda Burton serves as a receptionist and eligibility worker. She stays in the office, and therefore, the theory is that she's available to clients. It's called good customer service and makes Juney Bea smile. I'm in and out and often out in the "field" for what seem like days. Investigations usually take about forty-five days to complete. Much of my time is spent checking up on abusive parents, abused children and self-neglecting adults, as I need to monitor the home situation assessing risk. I don't want any kid or adult dying on my caseload when their death could have been prevented. I don't want to feel guilt. This insidious feeling of guilt runs high in Jewish and Italian cultures.

My co-worker Wanda doesn't have an ounce of Jewish or Italian blood running through her veins. She has no work ethic, no guilt, and no remorse. I know very little about Wanda as she isn't one to self disclose. What I do know is that she's single, about twenty-two. Pat Burton, Wanda's mother and Sally-Sue were roommates at Virginia Tech. Wanda's notorious for not being punctual for work; or for not coming to work; eating a thirty minute breakfast; followed by a two hour lunch; not returning phone messages and sitting at her desk twittering on the Internet.

Wanda and I don't communicate. To be honest, I'm a little scared of the Bitch. At times, I have witnessed her glaring at me. Talk about a hostile work environment. Hostile work environments usually have something to do with sex. This doesn't. It's called fearing for one's life, which in turn, in my book, labels it hostile.

The only tiny piece of gossip that I was able to wheedle from my mom, who knows Sally-Sue and Juney Bea well, is that Wanda's mother, Pat and Sally-Sue when they were roommates at Virginia Tech, during a summer break, hitch-hiked to San Francisco in 1967. History books describe the "Summer of Love" as a season of free love, free-drugs, togetherness, and peace. About 100,000 earthy folks converged onto a neighborhood called Haight-Ashbury. Mom says that Sally-Sue and Pat returned to Tech with a dazed look smelling of Patchouli Oil also known as Petruly Oil. Mom explained that this oil was worn by dirty Hippies. The Hippie didn't shower and would use Patchouli Oil to mask the scent of pot and body odor. Hippies loved wearing this. Come to think of it, I think to this day Sally-Sue still wears this oil. I know what it smells like. Mom used it when she masqueraded as Hippie for a Halloween costume party. Although I smoke marijuana, I do bathe daily and the smell of Petruly makes me gag.

At times I catch Wanda staring into space. I wonder if LSD or the "Summer of Love" did something to her mom, causing Wanda to have a brain malfunction. At first I thought that Wanda had a seizure disorder, as she would sit at her desk staring, not answering phones, oblivious to any chore tied to work. Clients sat in the waiting room for a good hour while Wanda was having a staring into space session. Sometimes she took from her pocket a Knight from the chess game in the waiting room and twirled it around in her fingers. My guess is that she's tied to some gang. Gang members sometimes carry chess pieces.

Wanda has the darkest eyes I've ever seen. She dresses mostly in black too.

Last month, after our agency's mandatory staff meeting in which Juney Bea spoke about customer service and dressing for success, Wanda caught up with me in the hallway and blurted out that she "didn't give" about Juney Bea's code. She proceeded to turn her butt at

41

me, point, spank it and blow me a kiss. I was stunned. This was the first time that Wanda had spoken to me in weeks. I've come to realize that Wanda will do as Wanda wants and Sally-Sue and Juney Bea will turn the other cheek, whether it's the cheek on their faces or butts. Black jeans, black T-shirts, black thong sandals until January. Then the thongs return in March.

Basically, I'm a one manned office. I like not being around Sally-Sue and Juney Bea and their nonsensical ways as for the most part, those in administrative positions are layered with dysfunction.

I once attended a workshop and the speaker stated, "90% of the population is dysfunctional." I raised my hand and brightly said, "Well if 90 % of the population is dysfunctional in some manner then 90% of those hired here are dysfunctional in some way." The speaker smiled and then moved onto another subject. I do believe that a large portion of those in the helping field have hidden agendas; although would like to think that I'm not a part of the 90% adding to the dysfunction of the Department of Social Services.

I've always wondered how Wanda got this position. What's the connection? Wanda has no eligibility background, has received little training and has no desire to do her job.

"Snap out of it girlfriend, my, you're deep in thought." Jodi says as we drive over the Chincoteague Bridge. Dispatch blares in her car directing officers to Assateague. Jodie drops me off in front of my office and takes off at full speed. I see her turning right onto Maddox and am wondering what's up. The Mamas and the Papas song is playing in my head again, "Monday, Monday, can't trust that day.

4

The phone is ringing as I enter the office. Wanda's not at her desk and it appears that she hasn't come in today. I grab the phone on Wanda's desk and it's Elizabeth Allen.

"Elizabeth, what's up?"

She's screaming. My heart begins racing as I'm wondering if something has happened to my horse, Trooper, an Arabian gelding, which has been boarded for a year at Elizabeth's farm.

"Elizabeth, I can't understand you. Did something happen to Trooper? I'm on my way."

I hang up. I scribble on a pink note pad about an emergency leaving the slip on Wanda's desk. I scramble around the office in search of the county car keys. In no time, I'm over the bay and turning left at Wallops. I arrive in fifteen minutes. There are several sheriffs' deputies' vehicles in Elizabeth's drive.

Bart Connors, Elizabeth's neighbor is hugging Elizabeth who has her face buried in Bart's chest.

"Bart, what's going on?"

"Someone has killed, shot between the eyes, Maryellen Holmes' horse, Star."

Suddenly, I have problems catching my breath. I lean onto the county car for support. I self-talk, *Francie, now's not the time to faint or have a panic attack. Deep breathe; you can make it through this.*

"I think that I need to call my supervisor and take the rest of the day off."

I open the door to the county car and find the county cell phone. I speed dial my supervisor's number but only a message comes on. I click it off and then speed dial, Erma Watson, Sally-Sue's watchdog.

"Erma, this is Francie, I'm trying to get a hold of Sally-Sue."

"She still hasn't come into work. After she received the U-turn ticket, Sally-Sue was determined to get her McDonald's meal. She drove up to the window and got a flat. She's at Earl's garage."

"Erma, I'm so sorry to hear about Sally-Sue, but something's happened where I have my horse boarded. Someone murdered one of the horses. Shot it between the eyes. I'm too upset to work any longer today. I'm taking the rest of the day off."

"Oh my God! Since Sally-Sue isn't here, you need to call Juney Bea as you know we just got lectured and warned about not following protocol. By the way, what happened at Friendship Place?"

45

"Everyone was present for the head count. So far it's a mystery as to who this elderly gentleman is."

I speed dial Juney Bea, dreading any form of conversation. She answers on the third ring much to my dismay, as I wanted to leave a message.

"Ms. Karring, this is Francie Batista over in Chincoteague. I need to take the rest of the day off as somebody's murdered a horse where my horse is boarded. I'm too upset to work. I also wanted to inform you that earlier today I went out in the field with Investigator Burgess. There's been a murder of an elderly man at Muddy Creek. I completed a head count at nearby Friendship Place to make sure that a resident had not wandered from this adult facility. There wasn't anyone missing."

"Francie, I really think that you should continue to work today. The horse is dead and you can't change that."

She can't be serious. I think that I need to be direct with this Hoe.

"As I told you, Ms. Karring, I'm too upset to work. The horse murdered was a pasture mate of my horse Trooper. Some sheriffs' deputies are here, the owner of Star, the horse executed is here and the person who runs the stable, Elizabeth is a basket case. Decisions need to be made as to the safety of the other horses."

"Well, go ahead and take off.   I don't understand what the big deal is.   Take care of yourself."

The phone goes dead.

Shaking my head and once off the phone, I walk over to Bart and Elizabeth.   Elizabeth removes her head from Bart's chest. She holds her hand out to me. We hold hands for a second and then release.   Elizabeth resumes crying and buries her head onto Bart's chest. I decide that now's a good time to break away from Bart and Elizabeth in order to check on my horse. I run to the barn.

On second thought, I detour to the left.   I decide that I want to see Star.   I want to say goodbye.   In the near distance I can see the image of Maryellen Holmes.   She is talking with two deputies.   The area is sectioned off with yellow tape.   I can see Star lying in the field.   I walk up to a deputy and identify myself by using my county ID.   The deputy permits me to get near to Star.   Tears form in my eyes. I stare.   Star has a bullet to the head, right between her eyes.   I notice that hooked onto her front right hoof is a wind chime. The wind chime is of a horse.

A scene from the movie *Jaws* comes to mind; Chief Martin Brody is receiving a neck massage from his loving wife on the beach just as Jaws attacks.   The beach chair moves towards the ocean, Chief Brody jumps out of his chair and

47

runs to the water's edge. Time stops for me as it did for Chief Brody. In the distance I hear a cell phone ring and Elizabeth's dog, Princess holds her head to the wind and howls.

Park Ranger Tony Jarrett enters Assateague Island National Seashore. Tony has the early morning shift. He's been working this shift for the past ten years. Straight days, Monday through Friday, no weekends and no on-call as this routine is what Tony loves, a consistent life with no surprises. Born in upstate New York, to two drunken and physically abusive parents, once Tony completed high school he moved far away choosing the Commonwealth of Virginia for its beaches and mountains. What's the State's slogan, "Virginia is for Lovers" and wasn't there a contest a few years back about changing the State song to "Sweet Virginia Breeze" by Robin Thompson and Steve Bassett? There's no other place to live.
  When Tony arrived in Virginia, he headed to the mountains working as an apple picker in Shenandoah and as a waiter, at an Italian restaurant. He saved every penny he had earned, applied and was accepted to James Madison University. With a student loan, and working part-time through college, Tony was able to make a new life for himself. He loved the university's small town atmosphere and

48

scenic views of the Shenandoah Valley. Tony initially majored in psychology, changed his major in his junior year and studied outdoor recreation and forestry. He continued with his education receiving a master's in forestry.

On semester breaks, Tony hitched to Virginia's Eastern Shore, falling in love with Chincoteague Island and Assateague. He studied the migration of birds, writing a published term paper outlining the yearly migration of birds to Assateague.

After graduation Tony landed the position of his dreams, a federal government park ranger job at Assateague Island National Seashore.

Ten years have flown. Still single, Tony has learned to love the wild ponies of Assateague, which is why he purchased his first horse, an Appaloosa gelding he affectionately calls Billy-Bob. Tony met Elizabeth Allen at a pony round up. Elizabeth loves trail riding and since Tony was looking for a place to board his horse, this arrangement has offered Tony an opportunity to ride with others and to know that Billy-Bob is well taken care of.

Each day in the early morning, Tony sits on the beach and faces east. He watches the sun rise and brings breadcrumbs for the sand pipers and gulls. They wait for him, knowing Tony's habits and routine. Tony's as happy as he ever has been, as he still loves his job. Not many folks can say that. He's never bored with the ocean,

49

birds, horses and the love of his life, co-worker Maureen Hughes.

Maureen and Tony's relationship has remained a secret for the past three years. They love their positions as National Park Rangers and don't want to jeopardize job security by their relationship, as surely one of them would be reassigned. They share their love for all living animals and enjoy walks along the surf, strolling down the beach long after visitors have left the island. They have remained purposely cautious and discreet.

After feeding the birds, Tony returns to the ranger station. Maureen usually arrives at about nine o'clock. He greets her daily with a large smile and a cup of coffee. An extra treat is doughnuts from Sugarbakers, a local bakery, better than Dunkin.

This morning Tony's a little late. He spots Maureen already sitting in the ranger station at the entrance of the park. Tony feels his blood rush and his heart skips a beat. As a joke he tips his hat to Maureen, winks and shakes his Sugarbakers' bag containing her favorite, a jelly doughnut. He walks over to the station to give Maureen a morning kiss. She's still as beautiful as the first time he met her. Tony tips his hat again. He sees that Maureen isn't looking in his direction. Fear goes to the pit of his stomach. She isn't moving; she's not smiling, and isn't waving. They had spent the previous evening together at her house off of Church Street and he had left her contented and happy after an evening of listening to music, drinking wine and making love.

Walking over to the station he says, "Maureen, are you OK?"

Maureen doesn't answer.

Toney continues walking and approaches her. Blood is splattered all over her booth. Maureen's been shot in the forehead.

Tony runs away from the scene and towards the lighthouse with his radio in hand. He uses his radio to contact the sheriff's department.

Captain Harold Winston likes to be referred to as "Chief". A heavy-set man with thick eyebrows and squinty eyes, he's sitting at his desk drinking his third cup of sweetened coffee when he hears of the shooting in Assateague. This is the third murder. *This doesn't happen around here. Something's definitely up.* He abruptly hangs up the phone and decides to call Ben Benson with the State Police. With six months to go before retirement, he's feeling his blood pressure rising and his ears burning. *I don't need this shit. This is all I need; some psycho-killer loose on the Eastern Shore and everybody becomes a vigilante. These folks will take matters into their own hands, like Charles Bronson in Death Wish.*

51

What I don't need is a bunch of vigilantes running around shooting guns from their porches at anybody walking down the street that they don't know. Tourists love walking along our sidewalks looking at all the homes, a pleasant place to visit, enjoying sea air, horses, ducks and Bill's Restaurant. Tourists won't be safe. Guns will be going off from front porches. With those thoughts, Captain Harold Winston stands up and kicks the trash can across the room. It hits the wall, falls, and papers scatter all over his office.

He's been trying to contain his anger. Known for a short fuse and at times coming close to emotional and physical abuse to his wife and children, he has attempted learning coping skills and anger management. He doesn't want to use profanity in front of the newly hired, twenty year old, female secretary, Brittany, who's cute and a knockout. She's added life to this stale office with her sweet smile and perky breasts. He would love to touch those breasts and kiss those full lips. *I don't want to get nailed for any type of harassment suit just before retiring. I really want my full pension.*

Chief really needs a drink, straight whiskey, a large glass; a few shots of whiskey will keep him steady. *I want to walk over to Bill's on Main Street and have a stiff one. Shit, I can't. I can't be drinking and meeting with Ben Benson. He'll know in a minute. Sonofabitch! This is going to be one hell of a day.*   Sighing, he picks up the landline.

"Hi, this is Chief Winston up in Chincoteague. Is Ben Benson in?"

Ben's been in charge of investigations on the Eastern Shore for eight years.   He's the best: reliable, honest, competent and solves murders. *He will make me look good.   What a relief.   I think that if these murders are solved quickly with Ben's expertise then I will look good just in time to retire. Going out in glory.   What an end to a long career.*

"No, he's in a meeting." Barbara Wilson replies.

Barbara has been Ben's secretary for the last six years. Good looking, stylish and quick witted. Today Chief Winston doesn't give a crap about quick wit.

"Barbara, please tell Ben that I have an emergency up here in Chincoteague. I really need to speak with him as soon as possible. I'll stay in the office until he calls."

"He should be out of his meeting in about one hour. I'll catch him before he leaves for lunch."

"Alright, thanks."

To hell with waiting to go to Bill's, I could do with a drink now, and the Captain reaches down to his bottom left drawer, unlocks the sucker, and takes a swig of Mr. Daniels, his favorite liquid.

53

Jodi arrives; her second murder of the day, and this is definitely not normal for this charming community. There are about eight vehicles, some from other precincts. Jodi walks up to the ranger's station and observes that Maureen Hughes has been shot between her eyes. She's holding a horse wind chime. The elderly man from Muddy Creek was shot between the eyes and was holding a horse wind chime. Jodi calls the captain.

"Chief, this is Jodi Burgess. We have a major situation. I'm at the crime scene at Assateague. Maureen Hughes is holding a wind chime. The dead man at Muddy Creek was holding a wind chime. Both chimes are of horses."

"I just got called from a horse farm at Watts Estates. A horse was shot between the eyes and attached to the hoof, a wind chime of a horse. Who's the highest rank out there?"

"There's Lieutenant Overbee here."

"Tell him to give me a call. I want him to secure the crime scene, leave a few deputies behind and everybody else meets here at 1300 hours."

"OK. I will tell him, sir."

Captain Harold Winston decides to visit Bill's. He grabs his cell phone, and tells Brittany that if Ben Benson calls to have Ben reach him on his cell. He grabs his light jacket and slams the door leaving it rattling. Bill's Restaurant is ringing in his ears. Over and over the name Jack Daniels is calling.

Tony Jarrett's in shock. Maureen dead, he can't believe it. Who would want to murder such a fun-loving wonderful human being? *I can't live without her. She is the love of my life.*

Lieutenant Overbee: "Mr. Jarrett I need to ask you a few questions."

Tony walks over to Lieutenant Overbee and turns his head to the right. Maureen's body is being studied by the medical examiner. He can't stand anybody around his Maureen, sweet Maureen. Lieutenant Overbee observes how distressed Tony is.

"Mr. Jarrett, how about if a deputy drives you home? We can talk tomorrow."

Deputy Martin is summoned and escorts Tony to his squad car. Tony sits in the back and cries uncontrollably. *Tomorrow will never come. I can't live without my Maureen.*

5

I leave the horse farm. I've decided to call it a
day. I return the county car to the agency and
decide to walk a few blocks to the grocery store,
which is across the street from one of my
favorite stores, Egret Moon Artworks. I wave to
the owner as I cross the street. She knows me
well. I love her store and spend half of my
paycheck, what little I get, at her store every
other week.

My intent in shopping is to purchase a bottle
of red wine and some cheese and crackers. I
plan to drink and cram as much food into my
mouth as I can. I'm so stressed. The wine will
relieve worry, and what the heck; some pot will
ease anxiety. I think I'll listen to some country
music too, like Toby Keith's *Beer for my Horses*.
Unlike mom, who's a Dead Head and Dylan
freak, I like country music, although I do love
guitarist Keith Richards of the Rolling Stones
and a group called Lamb of God from
Richmond.

I feel like I'm in a daze. I enter the food
store, come around the aisle and collide with
James Parker, Elizabeth Allen's boyfriend.

"Francie, you really look like you're frazzled. What's wrong?"

"Has Elizabeth called you?"

"I haven't had my cell on. The battery's low so I'm charging it."

"I think that you should call her as something's happened at the farm and I don't feel that I should be the person to tell you."

"Is Elizabeth alright?"

"Yeah, but you need to call her. Look, I have to go."

I pay quickly. I'm a woman on a mission. I want to get home, drink some wine, smoke a little reefer, eat and relax. This event at the horse stable has been too much for me.

As I'm leaving the grocery store, I spot one of my clients, Al Sharpe, who's not the brightest bulb on the Christmas tree.

"Hey, Dude!"

I can't believe that he's calling me Dude. I need to ignore his salutation and him.

"Oh, hello Mr. Sharpe, how are you today?"

"I would be fine if you hadn't called the building inspector on me and removed my two kids."

I watch my voice tone, keeping it low and even. "Mr. Sharpe, we've gone over and over this. Your house was falling apart, had roaches everywhere, especially in your kids' ears. I tried to work with you but you gave me no choice but

57

to remove your children. Hopefully, you're working with the building inspector so that you can have a safe place for Rita and Jackson when they are returned to your care."

"I'm working on a service plan as you call it. Rob Sawyer with buildings has given me a thirty-day to-do list. You said that I could have visitation with my kids. You haven't made arrangements for a visit. Maybe you can come over. I'll show you that there are no roaches. I'll even prove to you that there are no roaches in Rita and Jackson's beds."

"I don't think so. Look, I need to go."

As I'm about to walk out of the store, Diane Tate sees me and waves. I try to divert my eyes and lower my head, but it doesn't work.

"Francie, I'm feeling so much better since I spoke with you on Friday. It makes me feel good to have someone to talk with. You understand my situation. I wish that my mother did. It's not like this stuff that happens to me I plan. At least you listen and comprehend. My mother doesn't. Can I come by this Friday again at about two?"

I hate Friday appointments. Doesn't she realize that I just want to get the hell out of Dodge for the weekend? "I'm happy that you're feeling better. I'll mark you in on my calendar for this Friday. I've got to go, and I'll see you in four days."

As I step off of the sidewalk to cross the street, I hear a loud horn.   As I look left a truck has narrowly missed running me over. The person behind the wheel looks like Wanda Burton, Chincoteague's model eligibility worker. The truck, an old 1993 Dodge Ram, has the body of a real clunker. It looks to me that she's smiling.

Life is totally out of control and insane. I need to go home before I get myself run over by Wanda, or murdered by this wind chiming free roaming lunatic or raped by my disgusting client, Al Sharpe.

I return to my office, grab my bag and make a mental note to myself that Wanda isn't here. I leave another message for her, attaching it to my first note of the day. I place more food out for the cats, get on my bike, placing my goodies in my bike's basket, and in no time I'm making a left onto Main and a right onto Maddox. I rush home, jumping off of my bike and letting it fall to the ground.   The handle bar hits my knee causing me to wince in pain. I kick the bike in anger.   Rubbing my knee, I retrieve my recent purchases and as I leave, my pants catch on the bike pedal and I trip. I give the bike another kick.

I feel a little better although I know that I don't usually act in this manner unless I'm having a meltdown.   I need a drink to calm my nerves. I

59

run up the stairs to my second floor apartment, struggle with my apartment key and finally the door opens. I slam the door and exhale, leaning my body against my front door.

Sophie greets me and rubs herself against my legs. She can be a real pain in the ass when she wants to be. I put some food in her bowl hoping that she'll leave me alone. Pouring a glass of Zinfandel, I get excited about the thought of rolling a joint. I go to my stash, located in the kitchen. I have a Biscotti jar where I store my pot. This colorful jar is definitely a highlight to my drab kitchen. It sits positioned on top of the refrigerator out of reach to visitors. I wouldn't want an unaware guest to think that delicious Biscottis were in the jar and plunge their hand in, coming out with a plastic bag of pot.

I take a swig of wine, roll a joint and quickly light up and inhale. The cheddar cheese comes next. I slice the cheese into pieces, open a box of crackers and exhale. I remember some French dip in the refrigerator and a bag of potato chips in the pantry. I proceed to dip, devour, gulp and smoke. *This is emotional eating at its finest. I need it and I'm making it mine. To hell if I get love handles on my hips, and have shortness of breath from smoking pot. I'll worry about love handles and lung problems in my old age. That's if I see my old age.*

My cell phone rings and I look at the number. It's mom. I do want to speak with her however; not while high though. She would know right away. Mom can smell the stuff over a cell phone connection. This one of a kind scent can waft clear across Virginia. I ignore the call. It's easy.
I continue to eat greedily, smothering my mouth with the delicious tastes of chips, wine and pot. This has been an unbelievable day. I wonder what happened over at Assateague. Maybe I should call Jodi and see what's up. Maybe I better not call Jodi, as I've been smoking. She might realize that I don't sound the same or something. My habitual pot smoking I've never shared with Jodi, couldn't, wouldn't, after all she's a cop.

I decide to take a nap. I've promised Elizabeth that I'll stay in the barn tonight to tend to the horses, watching and listening for the slightest noise. I don't have a plan if the killer returns. I do own a gun, and intend to take it with me. It's a small revolver. I've never shot a gun before. I purchased it from a pawnshop in Richmond, while attending a workshop about violence in America. All boarders are pulling shifts. I have the midnight to five.

I walk into my bedroom, undress, and snuggle under flannel sheets. I love the warmth of flannel sheets. Sophie joins me. She nestles between my legs. She isn't a pain in the ass after all. My last thought is of the killer. What do Maryellen Holmes' horse and the guy at Muddy Creek have in common? Maybe nothing, as the killer might just like to kill. Maybe the killer's a client of mine and was after Trooper and killed the wrong horse? Chincoteague is a small community and everybody knows that I have a horse at Elizabeth's farm. *This pot's too strong. I need to turn off my brain so that I can sleep. I'm getting paranoid.*

Tony Jarrett walks around his house. He looks at photos of Maureen and is beside himself with grief. It's too painful to think of life without her. He's worked hard all of his life and losing sweet Maureen isn't fair. He leaves a note for Elizabeth Allen giving her Billy-Bob, the gentlest kind spirited horse that he's ever known and leaves the note attached to the front door. He walks through his house and out the back door to view the sun setting. He spends some time looking at the picturesque sun over the Chincoteague Bay. There are a few clouds. One looks like the face of his angel, Maureen. Tony's pain is too much. He catches a glimpse of gulls flying over Maureen's face. Tony smiles, opens his mouth and pulls the trigger.

After running into Francie at the market, James Parker decides to visit Elizabeth. James drives an

62

old 1990 Dodge Ram.   It's a gas-guzzler, manual. He likes holding the joystick. It makes him feel powerful as he downshifts and floors the Ram.   As he drives over the Chincoteague Bridge, he looks right and sees his work crew resting. *What a lazy bunch. Wait until I come back from seeing Elizabeth, I'm going to dock their pay.*

James arrives at Elizabeth's and sees Bart Connors talking to her from a distance. He can see yellow tape surrounding an area of the back pasture. James is feeling his blood flow right through his body. He takes a deep breath, as he doesn't want to appear hot headed in front of Bart, who's just moved from Maryland to this horse farm community.

James opens the truck's door and proceeds to hop out of the truck, and as he does he steps into a hole that Elizabeth's dog, Princess, has probably dug. His good ankle moves to the side, almost over. *I would love to take my hands and strangle that piece of shit dog.*   James approaches Elizabeth and when she sees him, bursts into a fit of crying. Bart approaches with his right hand extended wanting to shake James' hand. They shake hands, with long eye contact.

"What the hell is going on around here? I ran into Francie at the market and she told me that something has happened."

63

Bart runs his fingers through his coarse black wavy hair and says, "Somebody's shot Maryellen Holmes' horse between the eyes."

James acts concerned. He never did like precocious, classmate Maryellen.

"What? I'm sorry to hear that. Elizabeth, I know that you're very upset. Is there anything that I can do to help you?"

"No, James. I have the boarders working shifts until this murderer is caught. I don't want to lose any more horses. I just can't imagine who would do such a thing."

Instead of Elizabeth seeking comfort in James' arms, she turns and buries her head in Bart's chest. James can feel his blood boiling. He turns and stumbles over another hole. *I can't wait to strangle that piece of shit dog.* He gets into his truck and leaves driving carelessly down the road.

Bart Connors moved from Maryland a few weeks ago. He chose the Eastern Shore for several reasons, as he loves the beach, eating seafood and riding horses. Bart's fond of gambling and this location is accessible to Atlantic City. Another motive for relocation is money. Bart has a great aunt from his father's side. He's hopeful that the old hag will die soon. Aunt Margo never married and has no offspring. She's a hoarder from what Bart has gathered observing the outside of her house and land. There are bits and pieces of stuff all over the yard and porch.   What's inside is probably forgotten money she's squirreled away in boxes, between mattresses and furnishings.   Since Bart's a betting man he's laying a bet that when his aunt dies that there's gold in her garbage. He plans to visit Aunt Margo again and suck up to her so that he can get a good look at what's inside the shack that she lives in.

Bart frequents Atlantic City, and especially enjoys playing Black Jack, drinking and partying.   Women are an easy commodity. Black Jack is his game of choice.   About five months ago he was involved playing Black Jack into the wee hours of the morning.   He's good at counting cards and knew what was out and what was on the table.   Bart's an intelligent man, quick to take advantage of a situation whether it's with people or cards.   Nothing matters but getting what he wants. He told the dealer that he wanted to double down and it paid off. He won the $3,000 pot. Not bad for one night. With $10,000 down, Bart was able to purchase this small spread of land a mini horse farm right next door to adorable Elizabeth Allen.

At age twenty-five, Bart isn't interested in working. He considers himself a charming sort of guy, always having a woman around. Although during his high school and middle school years, the schoolgirls didn't give him the time of day. An outsider, who enjoyed taking the wings off of flies, didn't gain him many close friends. He was viewed as a freak, especially by the girl that was assigned the seat next to him in middle school. She reported Bart's behaviors to the principal, and he was mandated to receive therapy, which embarrassed George, his dad.

Too many social workers had been assigned to Bart, all to help him, even when he went to juvenile prison for malicious wounding. Therapy never helped, just made Bart angrier. George, Bart's worthless father, a psychologist, has a cushion job analyzing inmates committed to Maryland Department of Corrections. Bart's father may be a lovable sort of guy at work, but at home he had a poor track record, especially with Bart's mom, Hilda. George holds high expectations for his family. He's demanding and narcissistic.

Bart's parents have been married for thirty long years. Hilda's lonely and depressed and she drinks through her emotionally painful days. Her drunkenness is ignored by George. Hilda's loneliness has become her only friend. When she ran off with George after high school, her parents disowned her. As the years passed, Hilda lost contact with her younger brother and older sister. Her father refused to speak to her and would not permit Hilda's mother contact.

Bart's younger brother, Henry, is an ass kisser who sucks up to George. He's in his sophomore year at Maryland State University and is studying psychology. George is paying and paving the way for his son to be a psychologist, just like him. Henry's enjoying following in his old man's footsteps as both have Type-A personalities, are driven to achieve excellence and don't play in their spare time. Life's too short for them.

Life's too short for some unlucky bastards and Bart knows that he's a user. He doesn't care. He analyzes situations and enjoys playing life games and cards. Bart loves to manipulate and doesn't care about wrong. His actions are correct no matter what course he decides to choose. Bart's focus is on the here and now, and for the time being, he's decided to focus his energy on dear Elizabeth Allen. He's conveniently making himself available to her, and it's really pissing off James Parker. Bart enjoys watching James sweat, like the wingless flies, walking in circles on his desk for days.

Bart has grown to hate social workers. Francie Batista's a problem. She's smart and has good reasoning skills. She's one of those nosey kinds and most likely is the busybody of the Eastern Shore.

6

James Parker owns a local construction business called Parker's Odd Jobs. He and Elizabeth have been going together since high school, although James has cheated. He loves loose women, who like to get high and party. Elizabeth's an all American girl. She's the healthy and wholesome type, Mother Earth: no drinking, no smoking and no sex before marriage. What's a guy to do, but cheat; in order to get his needs fulfilled?

James lives with his parents in a trailer near Curtis Merritt Harbor. His parents purchased a small trailer, pay a lot fee, and have added on to their trailer through the years. Although it has an awkward appearance, James is comfortable and has added a bedroom and bath for himself.

James loves the south side of the island. There are fewer tourists and the area in its own way is attractive. He enjoys fishing, and envisions owning a fishing boat to charter excursions. Operating a construction business has its ebb tides, and it has become more difficult each day dealing with the idiots that he hired to build this new bridge.

James once imagined his life as a Chincoteague sheriff. This dream was shattered when he fell off of a roof six months ago. One minute he could have been a deputy, and the next minute he's crippled. Stepping off of a ladder, missing several rungs and landing on his ankle has been a pivotal moment for James. It has made him cynical about fate. He's in constant pain, with plates and bolts holding his left ankle in place. He limps throughout the day depending on a cane for extra support. Newly prescribed pain pills, drinking and drowning in sorrow for what would never be are James' daily thoughts.

Elizabeth says that his personality has changed. This pisses him off as she tells James that he was once a fun-loving, interesting, highly energized person. *What am I now?* Perhaps the face in the mirror is a shadow and Elizabeth's right. James admits that at times he does look unkempt, angry, and that he's moody. *Who wouldn't be?* He's taken up smoking Camels, too. James spends his days blowing smoke rings, driving around in his truck, checking on work crews and popping pain pills. He can blow two separate smoke rings, blowing the second one into the first. Now that's achievement. The nerve of Elizabeth giving him an ultimatum; clean up or pack up. These new habits, his all American girl won't tolerate.

When he crosses the bridge he drives up to the site where the work crew is. They are working on the new bridge. He walks up to Eddie Short, the crew supervisor, curses at him and punches him in the face. Eddie falls, and with his nose bleeding, scrambles back up onto his feet to face James. A bunch of workmen have circled the two. Eddie decides to walk away. He throws his hard hat at James hitting him on his left leg. James winces. He leaves, getting into his truck and peels from the work site, turning onto Main Street.

The crew's confused; they're shaking their heads. In this economy they all need their jobs. They walk back and continue what they were doing. Eddie goes home for the day. James decides to go to Bill's Restaurant for a drink.

Captain Winston slams the door to his office and walks across the hallway. He enters the conference room. Jodi has positioned herself by the only window in the room. She's recently purchased a yellow diamond ring from QVC and loves wearing it. Her fingernails have just had a manicure, light pink nails. She opens her left hand, stares at her diamond ring finger and moves it from side to side. The diamond catches the rays of sun and bling; she absolutely loves her new ring.

Jodi warily looks at the Chief and then decides not to make eye contact. He is looking like he's going to go off, and she doesn't want to be the recipient of one of his temper tantrums. Jodi can hear Captain Winston's heavy breathing. It's a sure sign of a fit of temper to come.

"I've just been notified of another murder. This time it's in Cape Charles. An unknown male, found behind Dollar General, was shot at close range between the eyes. A horse wind chime was hooked to the guy's nuts."

Jodi glances at the Chief. Her head's still down, although her eyes dart up and she catches a look at him through her blond bangs.

The Chief opens a packet of snuff and places a piece of sweet tobacco in the left corner of his mouth. Jodi, having worked for the department for the past ten years, knows what's to come. In a few minutes Captain Winston will spit into the Pepsi can and then go off.

"I don't need this kind-of-shit, six months prior to retirement. Nobody, and I mean nobody's, going on vacation. Nobody better call in sick until these murders are solved. I'm not going to retire after twenty-five years of service with any blemish on my record. All deputies and investigators will work twelve-hour shifts. All deputies will be visible. All radios will be on at all times and anything; anything that appears out

71

of the ordinary will be reported to me and checked into immediately."

Captain Winston, spits into his Pepsi can, finds the nearest trash can and for the second time in the day, kicks it across the room. He proceeds to screech orders at Brittany, his young secretary, who looks unraveled.

Jodi smirks. *It's good to see you worn-out; you're so young and pretty. Enjoy your day in the sun baby, as the wrinkles will come, boobs will sag and varicose veins will follow.   This killer needs to be dealt with fast. I've just paid for an all-inclusive week to Key West. I've had my leave approved. I can't cancel. I won't get a refund. I leave in one week.*

Jodi peers at her yellow diamond and the sun's rays, which had brightened this drab conference room, have left. Clouds have formed as a rainstorm approaches the island. *What did Bob Dylan say, A hard rain's gonna fall?* The sparkle's left the ring. Her polished nail has a chip.

Wanda Burton's, been drinking and snorting coke since she left work on Friday. She loves sleeping during the day, getting high and prowling about at night. Her favorite color's black, it fits her mood. Wanda's feeling hyped from alcohol, drugs and lack of sleep.   She's fuming. One thing that she knows is that her mother, Pat, got her this piece of shit job. Shit job it is: processing Medicaid and food stamp applications five days a week. What a thankless job. Sally-Sue Moon and Juney Bea Karring don't understand her level of job dissatisfaction. *My mother, Sally-Sue and Juney Bea got me this piece of shit job. I can't stand it and mom expects me to have it for life. She calls it my second chance.*

Wanda flips the top of her Miller and guzzles her beer followed by a loud belch. She decides to stay out of work for the week. She needs a break. Wanda's feeling manic. *Leave the mess for that pain in the ass, Francie Batista. What a Pollyanna type she is. I came close to running her down this afternoon. That Bitch forgot to look crossing the street. Wouldn't that have been the talk of the town, running over my co-worker? It would have served her right for not looking.*

Wanda replays the scene in her head. She throws her head back and laughs, then guzzles some more beer and takes a hit from her bong.

Wanda hears a dog howling. She enjoys living in Misty Meadows. The neighbors keep to themselves and it's out of the path of tourists. Wanda loves roaming the streets packing her 40-Glock. She reaches under her bed, rubs it, massages it, and gives it a kiss. My *best friend; it*

73

has never failed me, never talks back and doesn't expect anything in return.

Wanda continues to hold her Glock. She reaches for the remote and turns on TV. She sees Dr. Phil and flips him the bird. *I'll roam tonight when the natives are asleep.*

Lucky Lou Mann, a drifter, Viet Nam disabled veteran, has a post war history of drinking, pot smoking and schizophrenia. His daily leg pain causes him to drink. Cannabis relieves the noises in his head. Flashbacks are commonplace.

Lucky, is Lou's childhood name given to him by his sister Patricia. Lucky was able to stay away from his father's fists. Lou's father, Neil, a truck driving alcoholic, raised his family close to his parents' peeling wooden framed house in Bridgetown. Barbara, their mother, and Neil met in high school and as kids, attended Hungars Episcopal Church. The Manns on the outside looked put together: God fearing folks with plastered smiles. Inside of the house, Neil was a wife and child beater. His fists practiced on weekends. Sundays after church, he popped cans of Budweiser and assaulted family members. When Monday arrived, he kissed his wife and kids goodbye, leaving them with an array of discarded beer cans, bruises and broken promises.

74

WIND CHIMES   Teresa Adele Bettino

Lucky Lou's quick witted and fast on his feet, and prides himself on his ability to have escaped his father's fists and leather belt. Lou learned to detach himself from his psychological pain. He trained himself to be disconnected from the physical and mental beatings given by his father. He told himself that his father was non-existent.

Patricia wasn't quick, amble or bright. She usually had belt marks over her back for weeks at a time. At age 18, she left home, the day that she graduated from high school. Patricia told her brother that she would never come home again, not even when the old man died. Lucky Lou never saw his sister again. She left no forwarding address. Barbara mourned the loss of her daughter. She grieved, blamed herself and dreamed of life without Neil. Lou learned to never look back.

Lou rolls a jay and continues to think about his sister. Initially he thought that she would come for him... only one year apart in age, why didn't she wait for him to graduate from high school? They could have left together. He inhales and remembers graduation day. Their father sat proudly on bleachers looking like a peacock all puffed up. Neil had a large smile on his face as he joked with those around him. After the ceremony, Patricia returned home, went to her bedroom and packed her bags, placing her meager possessions in one large

75

garbage bag. She kissed Lucky Lou good-bye and left with the front door squeaking behind. She never said good-bye to their mother who was busy in the kitchen making Patricia's favorite dinner: meatloaf, mashed potatoes and cooked carrots.

Patricia opened the front gate, turned right and walked down Meadow Road. Five minutes later, mom called everyone to the dinner table: a table decorated with Aunt Margie's vase, with freshly picked wild flowers. Patricia never came to the table. Concerned, Neil climbed the stairs to Patricia's bedroom, found a card on the bureau, read it and returned to the kitchen. He proceeded to sit at the dinner table, leaving the note next to him. He didn't wait for Patricia to come to the table. Neil helped himself to mashed potatoes, didn't want meatloaf or carrots, and once the potatoes were chewed and swallowed; he pushed his chair away from the table and left the kitchen.

Mom opened the note. She read it to me. "Neil, eat shit and die."

In the distance Neil could be heard cracking a beer. Mom picked up Aunt Margie's vase and flung it onto the floor. Water, flowers and china scattered across the wooden floor. Two years later, riddled with cancer, our mother was buried in my father's family plot. Patricia didn't attend the funeral. Patricia didn't send a card.

Another drag, hold and exhale. Good old dad's vanished...the family house condemned. Another drag, and the winds are coming from the ocean...cooler air. Lou's voices are talking to each other. They're with him daily these days. Viet Nam's when they came, and too bad they didn't stay in Nam when Lou left. Shot in the right ankle by friendly fire, an Army discharge and the voices traveled with him to the States. Exhale and the wind moves Lou's ponytail to the side. Sometimes his voices are his only friends. Patricia was his friend and she's gone.

Lou enjoys roaming. He takes pleasure with the freedom of picking up and leaving anytime... no strings attached to anything or anybody. He receives a monthly check as thanks for a performance well done. The ATM card can be used anywhere. Not a bad life for a drifter, if only he could find Patricia.

Lucky Lou decides to hang out at the most southern tip of Chincoteague by Curtis Merritt Harbor, a little beyond it, near a transfer site. He loves watching boats coming and going. Having built himself a makeshift one-room house from a large box, he has positioned it between two grassy dunes. Nobody can see him as he's off the beaten track.

Lou loves living alone. This is just the way that he wants it; nobody needs him, not since Nam. He has everything: freedom to do what the hell he pleases and when the hell he wants. Isn't that what he fought for? Some good hash keeps the voices in their places... no arguing today, just sweet-talking.

Every day he takes a stroll to the transfer station. Tourists' garbage is good. The stuff that they throw out, not wanting to pack... it is incredible. Good food, magazines, clothes, you name it, it's easy to throw away and purchase again. America's a disposable nation.

Today, Lou's right ankle's hurting more than usual. He glances at the clouds and decides that a storm is approaching. He strolls to the dump. Lou sees and hears sea gulls above flying in circles. They are the loudest birds, and such vultures, always ready to eat. He steps on a clamshell and winces as he has stepped on it with his right foot. He looks down and something catches his eye. Lou limps over to the dumpster, and next to the dumpster he sees a gun on the ground.

He picks it up, hits the release button on the side, and drops the magazine. Lou racks the slide and one's in the chamber. Not fully loaded, what luck, a 40-caliber Glock.
He smiles, inhales. Sea gulls cry. He laughs. Lou's voices within his head screech in unison as more gulls join those above. He throws his head

back and laughs again. Exhales. Lucky is a fitting name.

When Patricia left home, she left for good. She didn't care if she only had sixty dollars to her name. Desperate to get away from her father, she hitched rides traveling west. It took several days. She slept in rest stops and approached truckers for transportation. Patricia knew that this was dangerous, although trusted that her guardian angel would protect her. For the first time in her life she saw mountains, beautiful trees and traveled through the Jefferson National Forest. Breathtaking sunsets over mountains with peaks of rocks and trees provided security for Patricia. Her father would never find her.

Patricia arrived in Montgomery County. Her intention was to attend Virginia Tech College and work her way through school. Her last ride with a husband and wife traveling to West Virginia left her walking along the streets of Blacksburg. The small college town surrounded by mountains and fresh air was all that she needed to feel as though she were alive.

Wednesday evening brought church activities and food at the local Baptist church. Patricia walked towards the aroma, fried chicken, meat loaf and fresh biscuits dancing through the evening air. She waltzed her way across the street and into First Baptist Church.

A woman smiled and walked up to Patricia.

"Hi. My name is Lisa Smith."

Patricia's taken aback and not prepared for introductions.

"Oh, my name is Pat Burton. I've just arrived in town and could smell food."

"Well, follow me as we have plenty of food."

Pat followed Lisa to the kitchen area of the church. About one dozen members were still in the kitchen cleaning up. Plenty of food was out in plates on the counter. Pat helped herself to fried chicken, mashed potatoes, tomato stew, and corn bread, and took a serving of her favorite, meat loaf. Lisa directed Pat to a small table in the corner of the kitchen.

"You seem pretty hungry. Have you been traveling long, Pat?"

"Yes. I've just graduated from high school and found it necessary to get away from my father. I plan to work during the summer and attend Virginia Tech in the fall."

"Do you have family here?"

"No."

"You have wonderful plans dear, but I'm concerned that you have no family around here. How are you going to support yourself?"

"I'm determined. I want to thank you for dinner, Ma'am."

Pat got up carrying her tray with the intention of cleaning her plate and utensils and leaving.

80

"Listen, Pat. I didn't mean to pry. I'm just concerned about your well-being. I don't think that you have anywhere to go to tonight. It's late and I'm sure that you have had a long day. Why don't you stay with my husband, Richard and me? Our daughter's recently gotten married and we have a spare room. I can't stand the thought of you not having a place to stay."

"Why don't I think about it, Lisa? If you could give me your phone number, I could call you if I can't find a place to stay."

"Well of course dear. Here's my husband's card. Richard is the minister for this church and we live next door to the church."

Pat gave Lisa a hug of thanks and left. She instantly felt at home with Lisa, although didn't want to impose, however; really didn't have a plan as to where she was going to live. Her $60 wasn't going to go too far.

Pat spent her first night in Blacksburg under a tree, trying to sleep, but too afraid to close her eyes. She felt guilty for lying about her last name and felt that meeting Lisa was a blessing and surely a sign from God. After spending a scary, sleepless night, the very next morning Pat called Lisa. The offer was still good.

Pat lived with Richard and Lisa Smith in her freshman and senior year. During Pat's sophomore and junior years she lived on campus with Sally-Sue Moon. Pat worked her way through college as a part-time waitress at Anthony's Pizza. She majored in horticulture and learned that she was passionate about tending to gardens, especially English gardens. Pat was determined never to return to the Eastern Shore. That part of her life was gone although at times she missed her brother, Lou.

7

The second meeting of the day takes place in the sheriff's conference room. Jodi finds her place and shines her diamond onto the wall. *It's the little things in life that makes one happy.*

The Chief's face and ears aren't red anymore, which Jodi sees as a good sign. Even Brittany in her hot pink dress doesn't look as stressed.

Chief Winston: "I would like to introduce you to Ben Benson. A few of you who have been here for the past ten years probably know him. In fact you may have worked with him on difficult cases. I called him earlier today as we have a killer on the loose. We need the State Police involved. I'll let Ben take over."

"I'm not going to say that it's good to be back. It's never good to be back under these circumstances. I'm stationing eight of my officers in Chincoteague for an indefinite period. We have a profiler available so anybody with any information will be able to speak with Trooper Goode."

Jodi's listening intently as she's very concerned. Not only is she concerned as to the safety of residents, but also this murderer needs to be located, arrested, and charged. *This has to be solved in one week or I'll lose my vacation in Key West.* Jodi glances at her ring, finds another sunspot and watches it gleaming. *This ring's a present to me for all of my hard work and long hours. My yellow diamond, shimmering describes how I want my vacation: flashy, sparkly, and fun.*

Chief Winston: "Tonight we start 12-hour shifts. Get with your partner and get organized. Be careful."

Andy Walsh is Jodi's partner. He's lived in Chincoteague all of his life. His wife Linda and he were high school sweethearts. Andy has been Jodi's partner for the past three years. He's competent, responsible and dependable. Jodi trusts him with her life.

Andy approaches Jodi outside of the precinct. Jodi notes that he's looking a bit stressed.

"Jodi, tonight is my wedding anniversary, and Linda and I plan to go out to Wright's Seafood Restaurant. We've had this planned for weeks. I have a babysitter for little Sammy."

"OK Andy, no problem. Let's just take a moment and plan our shifts. I will cover for you, and you can cover some time for me as I had planned to have my hair cut on Tuesday afternoon. So, what we'll do is even the shifts."

Jodi says smiling as she shows Andy her latest piece of jewelry.

"That's really a pretty piece. I got Linda a locket for our two-year wedding anniversary. I placed a picture of Sammy inside."

"I bet that Linda will like the locket and having the photo of Sammy will mean a lot to her. Well, I better go and do a few things before my shift starts. Contact me on my cell phone when you are able to relieve me. Have a really good evening Andy."

"Thanks Jodi. I will make it up to you."

"Andy, we need to work long and hard on this situation. You know that I've already paid for my week's vacation in Key West. I can't get my money back."

"We'll nail this sonofabitch to the wall Jodi."

My cell awakens me; I can see the number and name, MOM. I'll just ignore it. I look at the clock and realize that it's about 11:30 and I'm supposed to start the midnight shift at the barn. I dress, grab John Sandford's book, *Invisible Prey*, about elderly women getting bludgeoned to death, along with random robberies, which makes me think about these two murders. Could robbery have been the motive? Somehow I don't think so.

Leaving my apartment I pack my revolver in a backpack, grab some potato chips shoving

85

them into my mouth and take a swig of the remnants of Zinfandel. I'm ready for my barn shift. I'm to relieve Elizabeth.

I arrive at the farm. No lights are on in Elizabeth's house. I drive straight to the barn. Every light is on. The security lights are lighting near pastures. I open two sliding doors and spot Elizabeth sleeping on a lounge chair with Princess sleeping between her legs. I nudge and call her name softly as I don't want to alarm her in any way. She awakens. Elizabeth is groggy and rubbing her eyes.

"Oh, hi, Francie. Is it time already?"

"Yep. How are you feeling?"

"Dr. Smith called in a prescription and I have taken two pills. I feel totally relaxed. Bart has agreed to relieve you. Then I will be up and in the barn like usual at six o'clock. Bart's been really nice. It's strange, I never made time to introduce myself and to get to know him before now."

I'm thinking, oh no, where is this leading? What about James? I watch her move. Princess jumps off of her lap. Elizabeth stretches and leaves the barn heading for her house. Princess is at her heels, eagerly wagging her tail. She's ready for bed as it's been a long day.

I sit reading for about an hour. The horses are contented, some eating hay, others sleeping with

their back hoof tilted, a sign of their fight or flight history, as the foot tilted is accessible for a good kick to any predator. In the distance I hear a dog barking. I don't think that it's Princess, however; it stirs my curiosity. I must have dozed off as the *Invisible Prey* book that I was reading is on the barn floor. *Shit, I've lost my page. I hate that.*
Hemingway the barn cat jumps off of my lap. Normally, very friendly in nature, he growls as the dog in the distance begins to howl. *Most likely a hunting dog has picked up a scent of a rabbit.*

As I become a little fearful, I think that I can hear some footsteps by the barn doors. I decide to hide in one of the horse stalls. I pick my horse, Trooper, as I know that he won't be kicking or trying to bite me. I notice that he has thrown a shoe; *damn I'm gonna have to call Ross, my blacksmith.*

I crouch by the stall door. I reach for my gun in the pocket of my hoodie and realize that I have left the sucker in my backpack, which is lying by the lounge chair. The horses start to snort. I pick up Trooper's shoe. The figure's all in black. I throw the shoe as the intruder approaches Trooper's stall. As I throw, I scream, hitting the intruder in the head with the metal shoe.

"Shit…it's me!"

I peer from the stall: "For God sakes, James, you scared the crap out of me."

"I'm sorry. You hit me with the horseshoe in my head. Are you nuts?"

"Where's your cane and why are you wearing a black Hoodie? You're lucky that I didn't shoot you. Why would you show up unannounced when this murderer is on the loose?

"What's it to you if I have a cane or not? I thought that I'd be a nice guy for a change and check up on the place. I didn't know that you were going to be in the barn. I figured Elizabeth would be watching the horses and wanted to spend some time with her. I've tried to reach her several times, but she isn't answering the phone and her lights are out. I guess since she isn't here that she's probably sleeping."

"If you want, I can relieve you as it's almost three o'clock and I know that you need to go to work tomorrow."

Just as I was about to reply Bart Connors comes inside of the barn.

"Hello, James. Hi, Francie. It's shift changing time."

"Bart, if you would like for me to take your shift, I can, as I need to spend some time with Elizabeth today. She's pretty upset."

"No thanks. I don't mind doing this and I promised Elizabeth that I would be here when she comes to the barn to feed-up."

James turns, and leaves in a huff.

His last words leaving the barn were "that Hoe, that Bitch."

The Dodge Ram screeches down the road.

Within the darkness the mysterious dog howls again.

Bart Connors has made himself available. He's present for Elizabeth's needs. She's weak and he loves to find weakness. That's what makes vulnerability.

She's making some decent money boarding and training horses too, although not the gambling type; she's a saver, saving for a rainy day. Since the murder of Star, Elizabeth has started to depend on Bart more and more. They have been eating meals together and taking walks along the bay. This is exactly where Bart wants Elizabeth, dependent on him.

Bart's enjoying watching James squirm. James and Elizabeth have dated since high school. They're islanders. James has made himself too comfortable depending on Elizabeth. She's his balance. He's juggling to find his sense of balance since his accident. James' once stable life is unsteady and with his addiction to pain pills and alcohol, this unsteadiness is getting harder each day. James has that angry look and Bart feels it and wants to use that rage. Bart considers himself an opportunist and this is the time to move. James is a loser and Elizabeth's too good for him.

It's Tuesday and I'm late getting up and late getting to work. I arrive and Wanda hasn't come in yet. I'm starting to get concerned about what has happened to her given the murder of the guy at Muddy Creek and Star, the Quarter Horse.

I decide to give Sally-Sue a call. She doesn't answer. There's a day old voice message saying that she will be in about noon. I dial Erma Watson, her secretary.

"Erma this is Francie. I'm looking for Sally-Sue as Wanda didn't show for work yesterday. I am wondering if she's OK."

"Sally-Sue's in Newport News for a regional meeting. It's a meeting about the new program called, No Wrong Door. You know, the current trend is to let folks out of nursing homes, to return them to the community."

"Are you sure, it's called No Wrong Door as Sally-Sue sent an e-mail and called it No Back Door? I thought that the State was going to plug-in some services for these folks leaving?"

"I told Sally-Sue to stop calling it, No Back Door, as she keeps confusing everybody. You know Sally; she loves to be involved with everything going on. She hates when she's not being first with some bright idea or new program."

90

What an ass kisser. "I tell you one thing, if the State is thinking of discharging the demented man that I just placed at End of Life Nursing Home, then that State worker needs to find services to maintain him in the community. Without family support, it isn't gonna work."

"I know what you're saying Francie, but Sally-Sue is all enthusiastic about this new program. She's on her way to pick up this one hundred year old lady and place her back at her home."

"I hope she doesn't live anywhere near Chincoteague as we don't have the community resources to maintain her."

"The old lady owns a house in Wachapreague. All she's talking about is returning home and going fishing."

"OK, well... I originally called to let Sally-Sue know that I haven't seen Wanda. I'm getting a little concerned as Wanda will usually call and leave a message on my phone when she isn't coming in."

"I'll get in touch with Sally-Sue after lunch and give you a call."

My cell phone rings and it's mom. I haven't called her back and she's most likely worried. Just as I'm about to answer the cell phone, somebody's at the front door of the agency. I'll call her back in a few minutes.

Jodi's at the door, shaking a doughnut bag from Sugarbakers, a local bakery. She's looking tired. Her hair's in a pony tail and she has dark circles under her eyes. However; as she usually does, she's grinning from ear to ear. Through the window of the front door, Jodi flashes a diamond. I reach for the door.

"Oh my God" I exclaim, grabbing for her diamond.

"Do you like my new ring and how about my pink sweater?"

"I like the ring better than the sweater."

"Isn't it beautiful?"

"Jodi, you never told me that you were dating anyone, let alone getting engaged. What are girlfriends for?"

"Francie, I just purchased this for myself from QVC. I wanted a new piece of jewelry for Key West."

"It's lovely. What's it, a yellow diamond? You better get it insured prior to the trip. You look really tired, Jodi."

"I am. We're working 12-hour shifts and I pulled extra hours last night for Andy as he and Linda were celebrating a wedding anniversary. You look tired too, Francie."

"I am. One of the horses at Elizabeth's, where I have Trooper, was shot between the eyes just like the old man at Muddy Creek."

"I know. That's why I am here. I needed to see how you're doing and wanted to tell you that there was a murder in Assateague and in Cape Charles."

"Oh my God! Who was killed?"

"Park Ranger, Maureen Hughes, she was shot between the eyes. She was found holding a wind chime of horses. The unidentified man in Cape Charles had chimes attached to his privates. Don't repeat what I just told you."

"Gross, disgusting! Star, the Quarter Horse, had wind chimes too."

"I know. Francie, I really want you to be careful. Please watch over your shoulders."

With that said from my best friend in the world, I take a swig of coffee, although I need something much stronger.   I eat the entire doughnut in two bites and swish it down with some coffee. I'll be having an acid reflux attack in about five minutes.

"I can't believe that all of this is happening. This is absolutely unreal."

"I know girlfriend. Please be careful, I have to go.   There's another mandatory meeting at ten o'clock. I'll catch up with you later."

The front door closes and Jodi's gone. I'm in a panic mode mixed with a survival mode. Unfortunately, I've left my gun in my backpack at the apartment, as I didn't think that I should come to work carrying a gun. I'm freaking out, really having a meltdown. My heart is racing and I'm having problems breathing.

I place an urgent call to Kaylee with Chincoteague Animal Rescue.

"Hi! Kaylee. This is Francie Batista over at social services. How are you doing? Look Kaylee I was wondering if you had any large dogs for adoption. I would like to adopt two."

"Oh, this is great. Yes, we have a number of dogs for adoption. You can go on the Web site and check out all of our dogs for adoption."

"Kaylee, just tell me what you have."

"I have an adorable Shepherd mix about two years and neutered."

"Is he housebroken?"

"Yes."

"I'll take him, today."

"Tell me about another large dog."

"We have a female, Pit-Bull mix. She's a really a sweet dog, about three years."

"Is she housebroken?"

"Yes she is."

"I'll take her. When can I pick them up?"

"How about four today? I'll have them over at the Mall."

"Thanks, I'll see you then."

94

8

The door opens and I look out into the reception area.   Wanda still hasn't arrived.   I greet the person at the front door.   It's Ms. Miller a child protective service client of mine.   This means that she's either abused or neglected her child or children.   In this case she has neglected all three of her children by partying and leaving them alone at home.

"Miss Batista, I'm so happy that I caught you in the office.   I have something that I need to share with you."

"Come on back to my office, Ms. Miller."

Ms. Miller, a well-proportioned, dark haired woman with larger than average lips and tits is sitting with her legs partially opened wearing a short leather skirt.   She leans onto my desk placing her elbows onto it.   I move some of my cases so that she doesn't see anybody's that she knows and try not to look at her body parts.

They don't pay me enough for this bullshit.
"What can I help you with?"

"I need to go somewhere to dry out and to get away from Marty.   He has been slapping me around and the children have witnessed this.   It isn't good for them to see two grown-ups fighting, drinking and doing drugs. I would like for you to put Bubba, Sarah and Kate in foster care for a while. My mom can't take care of them as she just had a heart attack, and my father's in jail. Marty doesn't want them as he isn't their daddy."

This can't be happening. Not today. I'm really going to lose it.

"Ms. Miller would you like something to eat. I have plenty of chocolate. In fact, I haven't had lunch. Would you mind if I eat about five pieces or so?

This really can't be occurring. I will need to place these three ill-mannered kids into a foster home. And, God, the piles of paperwork that follow!

"Ms. Miller, how about if we work together and problem solve this. Do you have any relatives who would agree to temporary custody of your children while you're getting detoxed? The relative would petition juvenile court for custody, and once you're rehabilitated your relative would transfer custody back to you. The department has a program where your relative would receive a monthly check, and your children would be able to receive medical insurance.

"Well, I do have an aunt who lives down in Harborton. I can call and see if she would be willing to take them for about sixty days or so. You said that the agency would pay?"

"Yes. Why don't you think about this and call me tomorrow with your decision."

"OK. And thanks so much for listening."

I escort Ms. Miller from my office and through the reception area. Still no Wanda. It's raining. I hate Chincoteague when it's raining. I return to my office and finish off another piece of candy. The coffee's cold so I open a can of Coke and drink half without taking a single breath.

I really need to call my mother and let her know what's going on.

I speed dial mom and the phone goes to her messages.

"Mom, please give me a call soon as I need to talk to you, like this minute!"

I decide that I need to eat something substantial and walk across the street to Bill's for broiled flounder, coleslaw, and sweet tea. As I begin to eat, James Parker walks in, looking like the graveyard scene from Michael Jackson's *Thriller.* He appears to have been working as his jeans have dirt on them, and his construction boots have seen better days. He's in black and his face is pasty white. He's limping and really leaning on his cane.

"Hi, James. Why don't you join me?"

"Hey, Francie. Yeah, I'll sit with you. I came in from my work site as I felt that I really needed to eat a good meal."

"I'm here to have a balanced meal too. With all this stress, I've been eating tons of sugar."

"Hey, did you see us on the Today Show? We're known to the world. And how about the guy with a wind chime attached to his balls?"

"Gross!"

James is excited. He's animated.

I'm sitting with some psycho-nut case. I don't know what Elizabeth sees in him.

"I've wanted to adopt a couple of dogs for awhile so I called Kaylee earlier today. I'm adding to my family."

"Francie, stop lying to your friend. There's a run on large dogs at the humane society and local pound. You're scared shitless about these murders."

Look at this smirking idiot!

James orders his hamburger rare, fries on the side; ketchup's all over his plate. He's thumping the table with his hands. I feel as though he's staring through my soul. We eat in silence. I'm beginning to feel self-conscious of everything that I'm doing, including the need to let out a good burp due to a large build up of acid. I decide to change the topic of conversation.

"James, where have you been working?"

"I'm working on the new bridge with a crew. I'm also supervising another crew near Deep Hole. The work has been steady despite the economy."

"Oh that's good. Steady work." I glance at my Dollar General Store wristwatch and my lunch hour's up.

"Good-bye James, I really have to go." I stand up and notice just how rare his burger is. Blood is dripping from the roll and it isn't ketchup. *Thank God I'm a vegetarian.*

Before returning to work, I stop at a local pet shop called Captain Cody's Pet Boutique and purchase two dog collars and leashes for my new family members. Maybe I will begin to feel better with two dogs. I hope so. I had a dog growing up, but when I went to college, mom kept her, a loving basset named Georgie.

As I return to work, I hear a boat blowing its horn. For some reason this unnerves me, bringing shivers up and down my spine. Maybe grandma's right; maybe somebody is walking on my grave?

I unlock the door to the agency and flip over the open sign. I'm ready for business. Thank God no one's waiting outside. I go to my mailbox. Wanda's still not here. Sitting in the fax machine are two reports from the State Hot Line. One is from an anonymous reporter who's reporting about a malnourished baby; the other is

99

a report about a ninety-year-old woman who lives by herself and keeps falling. I decide to cover my butt and go out immediately on the malnourished baby. The old lady will fall whether I go out today or tomorrow.

I grab the keys and get into the county car. The family lives in Deep Hole, the northeast section of the island. Hopefully, I won't see James. I've had enough of him for the day. The interesting piece about Deep Hole is that there was a murder there in about 1885, when a man named Thomas Freeman shot Jennie Hill and her mother. He was in love with Jennie. Thomas didn't care that Jennie was only about fourteen at the time. How had he ever expected a fourteen year old to love him. He went nuts when he realized that Jennie didn't even notice him. He came up to her and started shooting. Thomas killed her and shot her mother, too. Then he turned the gun onto himself and made this a double murder/suicide. I do think that this is Chincoteague history, and if not, it makes a good story. I still don't know how the road ever got named Deep Hole. I think that it has a sexual overtone to it.

The house I'm looking for is around 5400 Deep Hole Road near the Timothy Hill House where the murders took place. I slow the car and count addresses. I see a weathered-looking clapboard one-story house located down a sandy road, a little back from the other houses. I drive up. I take a moment before opening the car door checking for loose dogs, roosters, ducks and any other living thing that may be of an attacking nature. I don't lock the doors. I may need to make a mad dash for it. The front porch is littered with empty beer cans and cigarette butts.

I knock on the door and no one answers. I can hear a baby crying in the background. I knock again and introduce myself. No one answers the door. *I hope that there's an adult in this house, or I'm going to have to get the police out here and go inside.* No answer. *Oh, great day! I feel another meltdown coming on. A crying baby and nobody's answering the blasted door.*

I walk back to the county car, get my cell and call Chincoteague Sheriff's Department. I speak with dispatch and request a deputy as soon as possible explaining the situation. I don't use the term "field" as the last time the dispatcher literally thought that I was sitting in the county car in a field. I approach the house again. The baby's wailing. I knock. No answer. Although I don't go to church every Sunday, I find myself praying. A prayer to Saint Anthony, the saint for hopeless causes is in order. I want somebody to be home and to answer this door this second. No miracle. Saint Anthony is letting me down.

Deputy Greg Franks drives up. I've worked with him before. He's another transplant as he's from New Mexico and speaks fluent Spanish. I don't need Spanish. I need a miracle.

"Hi Greg, nice to see you again, only I wish it wasn't under these circumstances. I'm here because the hot line received a report about a malnourished baby. When I arrived, no one answered the door, and I can hear the baby wailing. We need to go in."

"Just what I need, with everything else going on around here." Greg replies.

We walk to the front porch and Greg knocks identifying himself. No answer. The baby continues to scream.

"Francie, you stand behind me."

My heart is pounding. My tongue is so dry that if somebody asked me to spit, I wouldn't be able to. I'm standing behind Greg as he opens the door and am knocked over by stench. Death.

What happened after we entered remains a blur. Mr. and Mrs. Melton had been shot between their eyes and positioned holding a wind chime. The baby's standing up in the crib, screaming. I hold my breath, grab the baby and run. The baby's high-pitched wailing is in my left ear and I can feel my left ear vibrating. Once the baby's safely in the car seat, I walk away from the car and throw up my Bill's flounder. *I'm sure that I'll be in therapy for this one.*

102

Thank God they offer it for free as I will need all six sessions. Good thing I'm young and resilient. I don't even say good-bye to Greg. I catch a glimpse of him outside of the house, gasping for air. He has a cell phone in one hand, and a handkerchief in the other. I'll send him a thank you e-mail.

I peel out, burning rubber out of Deep Hole, hitting garbage cans with the side of the county car. Who cares? Thank God it's the county car and not mine. It's on the taxpayers.

9

I arrive at the agency, carrying baby and enter. Still no Wanda. I could use some help. There's a clothing closet stocked with clothing, diapers and formula. I decide to change the baby's diaper. I undo the saturated diaper. A girl, she appears to be about seven months. The diaper, I'll keep for evidence. It has ballooned with urine, has about three different types of bowel movements. Obviously, her parents have been dead for a while. Her bottom is beet red so I find some ointment and tenderly administer it. I put a clean diaper on the baby. She's starting to settle and is watching every move that I make. The powdered formula is good as I check the expiration date: add water to the powder; locate a bottle; cradle her in my arms and begin to feed. She grabs the bottle and eagerly drinks.

With hands free I speed dial Sally-Sue. She for once answers her phone on the third ring.

"Sally-Sue, this is Francie. I have a mess up here."

"What's the problem Francie? I'm dealing with a mess here."

"OK, Sally-Sue, why don't you tell me what your mess is then I will tell you what mine is. We can play show and tell." I say sarcastically.

"This one hundred year old lady, Elsa Powell-Smyth was asked if she wanted to leave the nursing home in order to return home and she agreed. It's all part of the state's new program called No Back Door. *She really means No Wrong Door; obviously Sally-Sue has opened the wrong door.* The psychiatrist at the nursing home deemed Miss Elsa competent. Miss Elsa lived all of her life in Wachapreague. She's a descendent of John Powell. He's the guy, along with his brothers, George and Henry who developed Wachapreague into a fishing area, farm trading and vacation spot. I dropped Miss Elsa off at her small-framed house, which is located across the street from Wachapreague Marina, late yesterday. How was I supposed to know that she'd leave her house to go fishing? It's really not my fault. If there's anybody to blame, the blame is on the psychiatrist. She was deemed competent by the nursing home's psychiatrist to leave. Anyway I picked her up, and returned her home with the understanding that supportive services for Miss Elsa would start in the morning. This morning she was found floating in the Wachapreague Channel tangled in her fishing line. Her fishing rod was floating alongside her. The family's hired an attorney

and is going to sue me, the county and anybody
who's had their hands in this case."

"Sally-Sue I'm sorry to hear about your
misfortune, but by now you know that there have
been some murders in this area.   In fact, I'm
holding a baby as we speak.   I just did an
emergency removal.   This baby's the only
surviving family member.   Her parents, the
Meltons have been murdered.   I don't know the
next of kin yet as this was my first contact.   I'm
calling you as I could use some help. Wanda's
nowhere to be found.   She hasn't called in. Do
you know where Wanda is?   Can you send
another worker to help me?   Do you have a
current list of foster parents?   I'm feeling very
overwhelmed.   I think the smell of death is
getting to me, as I can still smell death.   Can you
look into the free counseling sessions offered by
the county?   Do you need to sign off on
paperwork?"

"Look, Francie, I won't send anybody there to
help you.   We are all feeling overwhelmed, only
we don't broadcast it like you.   You figure out
who you need to contact for your counseling
sessions.   I'm giving this back to you.   I have to
go.   I'm getting ready to meet with the
Commonwealth's Attorney."

"Sally-Sue,   look,   I'm   really   feeling
overwhelmed.   I feel as though I'm falling apart.
There's no one to manage the front desk and do

106

eligibility, as Wanda hasn't shown for the past two days. Murders are being committed all around me. I have a baby in my arms as we speak. I feel as though I am having a meltdown. I feel as though if I started crying that I will never stop crying. I just saw two dead people and my friend's horse was blown away. I have a feeling that the killer wanted my horse and shot the wrong horse. This could be a client after me. First the horse, then receiving an anonymous child protective service report, only to find Mr. and Mrs. Melton murdered.

What if the murderer is trailing me around? You're my supervisor. Aren't you supposed to help me? Aren't we supposed to work as a team and be supportive to each other?"

"Francie we're all overwhelmed. Only you're the only member of our team complaining about how overwhelmed you are. You figure out what you need to do. Bye."

The nerve of Sally-Sue treating me in this manner! Wait until I tell mom about this shit. This must be how some poor schmuck feels right before he jumps. She's my supervisor. She's paid to provide leadership, although mom says, "Sally-Sue couldn't lead a cow to a barn." Screw her. Wait until she needs me for something. If she dropped in front of me, I'd step right over the Bitch."

I carry the baby over to my desk, open the bottom drawer and eat a chocolate granola bar. Once I swallow the bar, I travel to the file cabinet and proceed to look through mounds of files hoping to find something labeled foster care providers. I haven't completed an emergency removal before and will need to review policy. *Calm down Francie, there's a first time for everything.*

The baby's fallen asleep in my arms. I find a blanket and lower her gently to the floor. I decide to study what's inside of the file cabinet. As I walk to the file cabinet, I peer out the back window. I have a perfect view of the new bridge being constructed. I can see James Parker, limping around. He's still animated. His hand is pointing up to something on the bridge. He appears to be giving orders. The men are shaking their heads. Why is he still wearing that dirty black Hoodie? As if he hears my thoughts, James stops what he's doing and looks in the direction of the agency. He smiles.

I move away from the window, back to the file cabinet. I wish the foster care list was on the computer, but it isn't. Last time I needed a home, I found a list in this file cabinet. Hopefully, I put it back. That was about one month ago, when I placed Al Sharpe's kids in care. I locate a brown folder labeled Foster Care Providers. This one's tattered and not the one

108

that I used last month.   I review the list
recognizing a couple of families.   One family,
Erma and Ned Johnson is where I placed the
Sharpe children.   I decide not to call them.   I
don't want to stress them out with too many kids.
I'm hopeful that the other names on the list have
had criminal checks and have been approved.
Ironic of me to be concerned about criminal
checks when there's a lunatic running around the
Eastern Shore.   If I call and get a bad feeling,
then I will not place the baby there.   It will be the
fault of my supervisor for not helping me if
anything happens to this baby.

*Imagine, Sally-Sue not helping at all with this
situation.   Giving it back to me.   What's a
supervisor for?   I don't even have Wanda's help,
not that she's much help. God knows where the
hell she's been. I have no one. I feel like telling
Sally-Sue's supervisor, Juney Bea.   She's
basically worthless, too.   But then again, Juney
Bea and Sally-Sue attended the same college.
Nepotism, associations linked to college. Juney
Bea is famous for saying "Take care of
yourself," when the chopping block is coming
over your neck.   And saying, "Take care of
yourself," isn't that poor grammar?   Juney Bea
would never validate any wrong doings of Sally-
Sue.   How could she?   She's the one that hired
Sally-Sue.   Then, of course, they are sorority*

sisters, too. Is there anybody competent running the Department of Social Services?

I close my eyes and place my index finger on one of the names. I say a prayer to Saint Anthony again. Maybe he'll be able to help me this time. I call Ruth Applebright. Applebright, the last name sounds as homey as baked apple pie.

On the second ring a woman answers.

"Hello, Ms. Applebright, I'm Francie Batista, a social worker in Chincoteague. I don't think that I've met you, however; came across your name in our foster care providers' list. I've had to take, I think, a seven month female from a home located in Deep Hole earlier today and was wondering if you were still interested in foster care?"

"Well yes, Francie, is that the Melton baby?"

"Yes." I quickly reply.

"I know Sally and Ned Melton and baby Sunshine. I haven't fostered a baby in many years and would love to help out. This is all over the news. When would you like to come?"

"I have to be somewhere at four o'clock. I could drop Sunshine off at around three-thirty. In the meantime, I'll be looking for some clothes for her, diapers and formula. You'll be paid for your services as soon as I complete a case action."

110

"OK, I'll see Sunshine and you at around three-thirty."

Once off the phone, I gather some foster care paperwork, read policy regarding emergency removals and leave a message with the county attorney, Eileen Spark. I then pick up sleeping baby Sunshine, along with diapers and formula, and I leave.

Ms. Applebright, although a desperate choice, turned out to be Mother Earth. A pleasant woman, she welcomed Sunshine with open arms. Sunshine nestled her head into Ms. Applebright's large bosoms and instantly fell back to sleep. Talk about security and nurturance. Baby Sunshine will be well taken care of.

Social work is such a thankless and demanding profession. Nobody ever calls to say "Hi, I'm doing great!" Like Al Sharpe. He knows why I took his kids but blames me for doing my job. Then of course, social workers are supposed to be warm and caring folks. We are supposed to be understanding and compassionate. After meeting Ms. Applebright, who's warm and kindhearted, I've realized what's wrong with Sally-Sue and Juney Bea. They lack warmth and surely a set of nurturing tits. Ms. Applebright's warm, hospitable, concerned, sympathetic, empathetic and friendly. Sally-Sue and Juney Bea remind me of the song,

111

Cold as Ice, by Foreigner.   How they ever became social workers is beyond me.

Prior to leaving, I give Ms. Applebright my cell phone number and asked her to think about next of kin for me to contact. Ms. Applebright informed me that Sunshine is a nickname for Grace-Anne. I kiss the baby good-bye and jump off of the front porch steps, as I need to leave quickly in order to pick up my new family members.

Mom still hasn't called me and I look at my watch. It's nearing four o'clock. I return to the agency, park the car and walk across the street to the Mall. Kaylee owns a small shop on the left backside. She sells antiques. It's not unusual to see kittens running around the store. A donation jar is alongside of the register and has dollars and coins donated by animal friendly tourists. Kaylee is all smiles when she sees me enter her store. I shake the two collars and leashes in my hand and have a huge smile on my face.

"Francie, I can't believe that you're adopting two dogs. This is fantastic! Since the murders, I have placed five dogs.   The Shepherd is a sweetie.   He is eager to please and loves affection."

Kaylee brings from the storage room two wild pups. The male Shepherd is very friendly and runs to me with his tail wagging. I stoop down, pet him and he licks my face. The female Pit-

112

mix runs me over and I fall to the floor laughing. They both want love and kisses from me at the same time. It's instant love.

I give Kaylee a donation, place the collars on each dog, purchase some FrontLine to take care of fleas and leave the Mall with a dog on each side. We walk down Main Street and up Maddox to my second floor apartment. Feline, Sophie stirs at the front door awaiting my arrival. She catches sight of two dogs as the door opens and vacates. From the living room I see her scurry under the dust ruffle of my bed. I have great faith that all will coexist. Leashes come off and the dogs roam freely, sniffing around with tails wagging as they explore. Thank goodness my landlord, an animal lover, loves me. I pay the rent on time.

My cell rings and it's mom.

"Mom, you won't believe what has happened here. Have you watched the news?"

"No, I went to Charlottesville shopping today."

"There have been a series of murders and I had to go into a house and remove a baby whose parents had been shot in the head. I feel as though I'm having a meltdown. I have just adopted two dogs from the shelter. Star, Maryellen Holmes' horse was shot and killed...a bullet between the eyes, and this nut-job's leaving wind chimes. Mom, I'm freaking out.

I'm worried about Trooper. What if the killer is after me?"

"Francie, why don't you think about coming to Charlottesville for a week? You can bring Trooper, Sophie and the dogs. Do you have any vacation time? Why do you think this maniac is after you?"

"Because, I went out on an anonymous report and found two dead people and where I board my horse, Trooper's pasture mate, Star, is found dead. Maybe the killer shot the wrong horse? I don't think that I can get away. Right now, I have to pull shifts at the barn, as Elizabeth wants someone watching the horses every minute. She's so stressed that the doctor prescribed tranquilizers for her. She's unglued. Elizabeth can't stop crying."

"Do you want me to come? I could get someone to watch my horses."

"I don't want to put you out mom. Let me see how the rest of the week goes. I feel as though I'm falling apart. I tried to explain my feelings to Sally-Sue and she could care less. She basically blew me off. I was asking for some help as Wanda hasn't come to work for two days. I'm really mad at the way Sally-Sue treated me."

"She must be having another episode in her life that's spilling onto you. I remember how difficult she was during college days if

114

something wasn't going her way. Sometimes Sally-Sue would be having relationship problems with her boyfriend and she would take it out on everybody around her. Moody wasn't the word for her when life didn't go her way. Honey, try to come up for the weekend. If you need me, I'll leave and come and stay with you. Please watch out. I'm glad that you've adopted two dogs. They will protect and keep you company. Take them with you everywhere."

"Thanks mom. I love you."

10

I decide to take the dogs for a walk. It's a beautiful evening with stars and a sliver of moon. The air has pockets of warmth. I need to think of a name for each dog. As I walk past the decoy man's house on Maddox, I decide to name the Shepherd, Sergeant. It's a strong name. I need all the strength that I can muster. The Pit-mix, since Pit's have such a bad rap, I'll name Bella, beautiful.

I walk to the local high school and let them loose. Bella's, like a Mac-truck and runs over Sergeant within a second. She reminds me of a linebacker, using her body for blocking. Sergeant's quicker and runs away. Bella chases, but isn't agile. They run around the football field several times. After about lap four, with tongues out, they decide it's time to come to me. The game's over. I put leashes on the dogs and we continue our walk up the street. They love the combination of cats, ducks and squirrels. At a family gravesite, we turn and head home.

Walking home, I have a funny feeling in the bottom of my stomach that I'm being watched. I self talk that there's nothing to be afraid of as I have my dogs and gun to protect me.

Once safely home and with the door locked, playtime is over and everybody's ready for bed. Sergeant and Bella jump on my bed and curl up together.   I observe Sophie.   She cautiously makes her way from under my bed. She keeps her distance. I wonder how I will sleep with two dogs and a cat in a double bed.

I decide to take a bath. Usually I take a shower, but I need to soak in some hot water. I locate bubble bath, toss it in the water, walk into the living room and play a *Lamb of God* CD. Mark Morton's playing guitar to *A Devil in God's Country*. I'm head banging to the beat. *Lamb of* God members attended VCU, just like me, only they were smart and didn't major in social work. Good song and a good title for the shit going on around here. I pour a glass of wine and light a joint. There's nothing like a hot bath, wine, a joint and *Lamb of God*.

I must have dozed off. No music just cold water. I pull the drain plug; grab my towel and wrap my body into a pink terry cloth bathrobe, that mom had given to me as last year's Christmas present. My glass of wine is half full. What's the catch phrase? *Your glass is half full or half empty*? What bullshit. I drink the rest. Now there's no half to worry about.

I take a look at myself in the mirror. I've aged. My pixie cut needs a trim and dark circles are abundant under my blue eyes. I see a stray gray hair just above my forehead. I give it a yank. This job's aging me. I look like hell.

I walk into my bedroom carrying my gun. It's my security blanket. I place it gently under my pillow. I spray some lavender on my pillow and say my prayers asking God to forgive me for missing Mass this past Sunday and for listening to *Lamb of God*. Somehow, I feel that the name of this group is sacrilegious.

The last thing that I remember is Sophie jumping onto the bed and taking her spot on my extra pillow carefully avoiding the dogs.

James Parker shuts the door to Elizabeth's stable. The horses are in for the night. They are chomping on their hay. He has plans for Elizabeth tonight. James limps over to the house. The lights are on and he can hear some music playing. He knocks on the door and Elizabeth answers. Maryellen Holmes is visiting. He can see her sitting on a stool in the kitchen. He also sees Bart Connor as Elizabeth opens the door.

"Elizabeth, would you like to go to AJ's for dinner? They're having shrimp tonight as a special."

"Maryellen and Bart are over. We have plans to stay in tonight. Bart's cooking some steaks on the grill."

118

"I'd like to know if Bart's moving in on us. You haven't given me the time of day since Maryellen's horse was murdered."

"You know James, life isn't all about James Parker. I'm devastated by what has happened and Maryellen needs me. I really need some space. I want some space from you. You're not the same person that you were in high school."

"You know what! I don't need your shit Elizabeth. I don't need you. You don't even know a thing about this dude that you've befriended! "

James leaves and begins to walk to his truck. He stumbles on uneven ground.

James yells to Elizabeth as she shuts the front door.   "That piece of shit dog of yours, Elizabeth, you better keep a close eye on, as I'm gonna come over here with my Glock and kill her. He jumps into the Ram and pops a can of Miller. James reverses and backs into a chestnut tree, hitting his bumper.

James leaves the mainland, drives over the bridge and parks his truck on Main Street. It's about seven o'clock and *Beverly Hills Chihuahua* is playing. He pays, buys some popcorn and a Coke and walks in. Commercials are playing so he settles in, sitting on an aisle seat towards the back of the theater.

James is jumpy. James turns around and sees Wanda Burton. Maybe he should sit with her.

119

His loins are feeling hot and he needs some relief.

James gets up and walks up to Wanda who's sitting in the aisle seat, last row.

"Move over one so that I can stretch my bad leg."

Wanda Burton's pumped. She's coming down from a weekend of snorting coke and drinking. Of all the assholes to bump into, James, the loser of the island, and he smells of beer, has body odor and has a mean look about him. Wanda's pissed. She really wanted to sit and watch this movie by herself. The Chihuahua is so prissy. *What I would give to pluck the eyes out of that dog and then drown it.*
Midway through the movie, she feels James place his hand on her thigh. Wanda smacks his hand, tosses her popcorn and leaves the theater.

James watches the rest of the movie and decides to walk around Chincoteague. He's cranked. James limps to his truck leaning heavily on his cane. Once he reaches his truck, he cracks another beer, pops a couple of pain pills and gets his Glock from his glove compartment. He decides to take a walk.

James can't get his mind off of Elizabeth. He walks to the Fairgrounds and looks into the horse stalls. There are a couple of stalls occupied with Chincoteague ponies. He takes the Glock out from his hoodie pocket, aims and fires. *That one's for you, Elizabeth.*   James heads for Maddox. He wants to visit Francie.

Bart Connors has dinner with Elizabeth and Maryellen. He excuses himself early and returns home. He's tense.   Bart decides to go to Chincoteague to walk around. He loves walking around the island exploring. The southern tip, near the marina is one of his favorite spots. The view of Chincoteague Channel and the mainland is magnificent.
　　Bart walks in front of the movie theater. Ahead of him he sees James Parker limping down the street. He decides to follow him.

At about twelve, Sergeant starts to growl. Bella jumps from the bed and I jump out of bed and stand in the doorframe of my bedroom. My heart's pounding. I think that I can hear footsteps, but it's hard to tell with all of the noise. I walk to the bed and get a hold of my gun from under my pillow. My hands are shaking. Sergeant leaps from the bed and stands next to Bella. I don't think that the dogs are acting this way due to a bunch of ducks waddling across the street quacking. I close my bedroom door. I move Sergeant and Bella back and drag my bureau in front of the door. Sophie has disappeared; she's nowhere to be found.

She's not one for conflict. I grab my cell and flip it on. No charge.

Sergeant's growl is low and steady. Bella stands behind the bureau, stoic. I cock my gun. I hear my apartment door open. Somebody's in my apartment. Both dogs bark. I freak.

I begin to shoot through the bedroom door, and scream, "Fire...Call 9-1-1." Through the curtains of my bedroom window, I can see lights coming on across the street. I open my bedroom window and continue to yell,"fire". While screaming for help I notice a Dodge Ram parked across the street and a person limping up the street towards Assateague.

Sirens are in the distance. I wait. Fire trucks and police cars are outside of my apartment. I yell to them that somebody's in my apartment.

"Francie, it's me, Cindy Franks, you're safe, open your bedroom door."

"Deputy Franks, I'm sure happy to see you. I think the killer was in my apartment."

Deputy Franks spots three bullet holes in my door. She finds a slug in the living room wall.

"Did I hit him?"

"There's no blood, but I'm going to call Investigator Burgess and ask her to come and give this place a thorough going over. Maybe we can find a set of prints?"

"Jodi's a good friend of mine. Do you think that this person will come back?"

Tomorrow I'll have a dead bolt installed. I just know that this maniac is after me. Who would want to kill me? Maybe somebody on my caseload?

Jodi arrived in a matter of minutes. She really looked concerned that my place had been broken into.

"Do you want me to stay with you until dawn, Francie, so that you can get some sleep?"

"Do you think the person is going to come back?"

"I don't think so. Not with the two dogs and all the commotion."

"I think Sergeant and Bella saved my life. Talk about timing. This is my first night with them."

Jodi spent the next couple of hours looking for evidence. I feared that she was gonna find my pot stash, but she didn't. That would have been the icing on the cake for the day.

11

Jodi located me the next morning at my desk behind mounds of paperwork.

"I need to appear in juvenile court this morning as I did an emergency removal yesterday."

"I know. Don't you remember that you told me all about it early this morning at your apartment? I also heard about it from Deputy Franks."

Jodi smiles when she sees the dogs. Sergeant and Bella are sitting in front of my desk. She gives them a good pat on the head.

"Where's Wanda?" Jodi asks.

"Don't know. Don't care."

"How are you doing Francie? I mean really doing?"

"Not good. I think that I'm going to have a nervous breakdown. Look at me, I'm a mess."

"What can I do to help you, girlfriend?" Jodi says with big smile as she hands me a bag.

I peer into the bag and smile. Just what the doctor ordered, doughnuts from Sugarbakers.

"Thanks Jodi. There isn't really anything you can do to help me as I have tons of paperwork and still need to go out on an adult report from yesterday. There's some old lady falling and self-neglecting herself."

"I'm going to keep checking on you. Is your mom coming? You could probably use some homemade chicken noodle soup."

"Don't think so. Mom wants me to come to Charlottesville. As for soup, I'm a vegetarian. What humans do to the poor chickens!" I watched a video from a group called Mercy and cried for days. It makes you view livestock differently when you see this disgusting abuse taking place."

"Let's change the subject. I don't want to think about it as I like baked chicken and love scrambled eggs."

"Jodi, I am freaking out. I called Sally-Sue to tell her how overwhelmed I am, and that was before last night's ordeal, and she told me to deal with it myself. I can't. I think that the killer was in my apartment last night."

"I know. I have instructed the deputies to drive by tonight and keep a watch on you. I don't want anything to happen to you. How are Elizabeth and the horses?"

"She's a little better. She was able to leave her house and walk down to the barn without falling apart. Trooper has been neighing for his deceased pasture buddy, which is pulling at my heart."

"I'm so sorry."

With that said, I start crying. I bury my face in my hands. Jodi tries to console me, but I'm

125

beyond consoling. In about 24-hours, there have
been six murders. The last one with Sally and
Ned Melton has made me mental. I can't get the
smell of death from my nose. Smoking pot
didn't even help.

"How about if we get some coffee up the
street?" Jodi says as she places a leash on Bella.

"OK. Let's walk by Captain Cody's Pet
Boutique and ask Joyce if Sergeant and Bella can
stay for a few minutes. It may be good for sales.
Tourists love dogs and cats."

Joyce greets the dogs with much enthusiasm
as we enter. Bella sniffs out the doggie treats
and Sergeant enjoys sniffing Joyce's crotch.
Poor manners. Joyce redirects Sergeant and
gives out a hearty laugh. She showers the dogs
with hugs and kisses. The dogs couldn't be
happier as Jodi and I leave the store.

Coffee always helps me to feel happy. It's one
of my many comfort foods. We walk down to
Sundial Books and speak with owners, Jon and
Jane. Not only does the store have an art gallery,
but a small coffee shop, which is an added
attraction. Who doesn't like to sit, reading books
sipping coffee? Nice touch.

Fireman Luciano Levine, an Italian-Jewish
Jersey Shore Guido, recently relocated with his
Guidette girlfriend, Maria-Frances DeFore to
Chincoteague. Named after the famous tenor,

126

Luciano Pavarotti, Luciano's mother dreamed of her son singing opera at the Metropolitan Opera House as she sold hand-made quilts to pay for her son's singing lessons.

Unlike his mother, Luciano dreamed of becoming a fireman. When he arrived in Chincoteague, Luciano volunteered to become an active member of the Chincoteague Fire Department. Another dream of his was to become a Salt Water Cowboy. Once Maria-Frances and he located housing and both secured jobs at the Village Restaurant, Luciano purchased his first horse, a bay Arabian mare.

Luciano and Maria-Frances are happy with their new lives. Although Luciano never made it to the opera house, he does sing while waiting on tables until the fire siren goes off. Once the siren is heard, he's fighting fires while Maria-Frances enjoys life cooking seafood at the restaurant.

This morning its Luciano's turn to feed, muck and let out a couple of Chincoteague ponies that were adopted during the summer. The ponies are ready to be released and the owners are traveling to Chincoteague in the next week to retrieve their horses. It's almost the first week of November and the ponies need to leave the Fairgrounds.

He arrives at the Fairgrounds and walks over to the horse stalls. Luciano sees one of the ponies peering out of his stall. It appears nervous, as it's snorting and its eyes are large.

He walks over and peers inside of the next stall. The pony's down. He opens the door and sees blood splattered and a puddle of blood mixed with shavings. Luciano gags and runs back to his car. He calls the sheriff.

Chief Harold Winston's brushing his teeth, his wife of thirty years picks up the phone and State Police, Ben Benson's on the line.

Ginger hands the phone to her husband: "Yeah, what's up?"

"Another horse has hit the dust. This time it's one of the Chincoteague ponies that were stabled at the Fairgrounds. Fireman, Luciano Levine found the pony this morning dead in his stall. Some troopers and Investigator Jodi Burgess are at the fairgrounds now."

"What the hell's going on around here? I'm leaving now. I'll meet you at the fairgrounds in about fifteen minutes."

"Ginger, there's been another killing. Don't open the door to anybody. Nobody's safe on the Eastern Shore until this butcher is caught."

Jodi's tired. These twelve-hour days are getting to her and it's only been three days. Sleep hasn't been coming easily as she's wound up. Adrenaline is pumping through her veins along with all the caffeine that she's drinking to stay alert.

128

Jodi received a call to go to the Fairgrounds. The call came in at seven fifteen and she was due to change shifts with Andy Walsh, her partner, at nine. This killer needs to be caught and get the death penalty. *If I miss my vacation because of this maniac, he's gonna wish that he were dead, because I'm gonna pump a hole into the bastard. Thank God, Virginia has the death penalty.*

Jodi's busy collecting evidence with Trooper Goode. Both notice that there's no wind chime with this murder. Perhaps this is a copy cat killer or the murderer ran out of chimes?

The Chief pulls up, opens the car door and as he's getting out of his vehicle he spills hot coffee onto his crotch. He starts grabbing his crotch and screaming for a towel to wipe the coffee from his pants. Jodi holds back a grin.

"Chief, so sorry. Here's a towel. "

"Thanks. Get Ben Benson over here. I need to speak with him."

"So, what do we have?"

"We have a bullet but no suspect"

"Fuck."

A new day. Sunny, bright and Lucky Lou's happy. Yesterday was a good day at the dump. His voices are cheery. He loves having a gun again and decided it was best to bury it. Lou placed it in a box found on the beach and buried it under some sea grass, within a sand dune next

129

to his boxed home. Today, he's going to walk to Chincoteague Fast Mart and buy some cheap wine.

As he's walking up Main Street, he looks right and sees some State Police vehicles going towards the Fairgrounds.

He enters the Fast Mart just in time to overhear the clerk talking to a customer.

"Another murder.   This time it's another horse."

Lou listens as he's picking up some Mad Dog 20/20.

"Kaylee over at the Mall says that she doesn't have any dogs left for adoption. The last dog adopted was a Chihuahua.   It went to the eligibility worker, Wanda, over at Social Services."

"Walmart's running out of guns too."

Mumblings are in Lou's head. His voices are worried. He needs to pay for the wine and get the hell out of here. Lou buys his Mad Dog, a newspaper and A Win for Life lottery ticket for this Friday's drawing and heads for home.

Jodi meets her partner, Andy, and they discuss what's happened at the Fairgrounds.   Andy shakes his head.

"But this horse didn't have a wind chime."

"Maybe it isn't the wind chime killer, Jodi."

"This is so hard to figure out. The chief has called another meeting for three o'clock today. I'm going home to get some sleep. These twelve-hour days are killing me. Call me if you need me, Andy."

Lou doesn't get far down Main Street before he's picked up by a young sheriff's deputy. The deputy asks for an ID, and Lou complies. Voices tell Lou to take a hike. Lou rationalizes that it doesn't hurt to give the officer what he wants. If only the voices would settle.

"Mr. Mann, I see from looking at your identification that you don't live here."

"That's right."

"Where are you staying?"

"Nowhere in particular."

"That's really not an answer, sir. So I will ask again. Where are you staying?"

"Nowhere in particular. Listen. What's the problem officer? I have a right to walk down the street."

Investigator Andy Walsh calls for back-up. Within minutes, Officer Rainey arrives. Andy asks to speak to the Chief.

"Chief Winston, this is Andy Walsh."

"Yeah, what's up?"

"I've got this vagrant who's not cooperating. I'd like to bring him in for questioning. His identification says he's from Washington. He says that he knows his rights and doesn't have to come with me."

"Bring in the mother.   Arrest him for obstruction of justice."

Jodi can't sleep. She's tossing and turning in bed. *I've never been able to sleep during the day.* She locates the remote control on her nightstand and starts flicking channels: a rerun of COPS. Flick.   Animal Planet.   Flick. Her cell phone rings, and it's Andy.

  "What are you doing, Jodi?"

  "Trying to sleep."

  "I thought you might want to interview this guy I found. He's a drifter."

  "OK."

  "He's at headquarters."

12

Francie hears on local news about another murder. She calls her mother and tells her about the break-in and another horse dead.

Gertrude Batista's concerned about her daughter's emotional and physical state. She doesn't feel as though her daughter's safe. Forget about waiting for Francie to come here. Obviously, some loony-tune is loose and is killing everything moving. Gertrude needs to be with her daughter. *I'm really angry that Sally-Sue won't help my daughter. I know her well from years of social work in Richmond. She and Juney Bea are two peas in a pod.*

Gertrude calls her neighbor, Lonnie, a fix-it repairman, and asks him to keep watch over the farm. He'll come twice a day. No problem. As Gertrude's packing she decides to bring her revolver. By any luck she should reach Chincoteague in about six hours.

Life couldn't be better for Pat. Finally she's found the job of a lifetime, working at the Lakeside Botanical Gardens near Richmond. Lisa and Richard were the parents that she never had. She's fortunate that life took a turn for the better after she left home. It could have easily gone the other way. Barbara, had never been a mother to Lou and Pat. Barbara was afraid of her husband, Neil. He battered her in every way. What a depressing life her mother had. Why didn't she leave?

Pat's one major screw up in life was getting pregnant and not placing Wanda for adoption. She tried dormitory life for two years living with Sally-Sue Moon. During her second semester of her junior year, she became pregnant. Pat had been infatuated with Mark. He was in her literature class and picked the seat next to hers. Good-looking and he was a popular quarterback. Mark Adams had everything going for him, intelligence and handsome with a beautiful smile. Who could resist? She should have realized that he was using her for her intelligence.

Once Pat found out that she was pregnant, she approached Mark expecting commitment and got the opposite. He blamed her for this pregnancy calling it entrapment and refused to admit that this was his baby. He split the next semester, transferring to another college. Lisa and Richard were there to pick up the pieces and welcomed a baby into their home. They called Wanda a blessing. They helped Pat raise Wanda. For Pat, Wanda proved to be a difficult baby, problem child, rebellious teen and a pain in the ass as an adult.

Wanda's adolescence was turbulent. She had no friends and did not fit in with her peers. She got involved with a gang of thugs, became sexually active and started using drugs. When she started killing cats, squirrels and birds, Wanda found herself in a therapist's office. Marijuana and crack were used to self-medicate; used to balance her moods in order to feel normal. At times she was manic staying up all hours of the night, talking nonstop, giddiness and had some obsessive-compulsive traits like picking up discarded cigarettes off of the street. Other times, she slept for days and had no energy.   She refused to take prescribed medications insisting that she didn't like having a dry tongue and internal shakes.

Being a thief was Wanda's middle name. Nothing anybody owned in the family was sacred.   Why Lisa and Richard put up with Wanda and her, Pat will never understand. Perhaps Lisa and Richard's strong religious beliefs held solidly through all the adversity that Wanda created. Pat had difficulty finding the good in Wanda. She barely graduated from high school, couldn't hold a job long as she slept all day and prowled around neighborhoods at night. Wanda never fit in with any of the neighborhood kids. The killing and mutilation of animals was a grave concern for Pat as Wanda lacked remorse for any wrong doings, denied any wrong doings even when caught killing rabbits, cats, neighborhood dogs and squirrels. Therapy and a lengthy stay at Bon Air Juvenile Correctional Center came and went and appeared to have little impact.

Pat, deep in thought, was pruning an apple tree when she realized that the sun was going down. Visitors were leaving the gardens and it was time to call it a day. Pat studied the sun. Red. Tomorrow would be another sunny day. The sun was going down behind the herbal garden. Lavender could be smelled in the air. Tranquility ends when her cell phone rings.

"Hello, Pat. This is Sally-Sue. Look there's something going on with your daughter. She hasn't come to work in three days and won't return my phone messages. I spoke with Juney Bea and we'd like for you to come to Chincoteague to speak with Wanda. She needs to come to work. Her behavior is unacceptable. This doesn't look good."

"Sally-Sue, you can't expect me to drop everything and come to Chincoteague. I don't have any control over Wanda. Never did. She was born a difficult child. Perhaps she's off her medications. You know that she's finally agreed to get on some medications for her moods."

"If you don't come, I'm going to fire her. If you want her to keep this job, I suggest you come to Chincoteague right away."

"Well, if this isn't a crock of bull-shit. Of course I will come as Wanda needs to have a job. I can't and won't support her. What have you done Sally-Sue to help with this situation?"

"It's not my responsibility to see to it that your daughter comes to work and stays off of drugs. I hired her because of my friendship with you. After all, we lived together for a couple years in between your living with Richard and Lisa. Juney Bea listened to me and hired her because of our bond."

"OK. I will be in Chincoteague in a few hours."

Pat gathers her garden tools and contacts her supervisor. She can take the next couple of days off. She goes to her Lakeside home, packs an overnight bag and gets on her motorcycle heading out of Richmond by way of I-64.

I have just returned to the office and it's Wednesday. Still no Wanda Burton, but at this point I really don't care. Sally-Sue has called and wants me to meet her in Newport News for a regional meeting about No Wrong Door. She's getting sued for taking that old lady out of the nursing home. It can sure sour a program fast, having the first participant die.

I decide to wait another day to go out on the adult report about Margo Newman falling as Sally-Sue has made this mandatory for me to attend. I don't know why she feels that I need to be there. I hate regional meetings and I'm not about to remove anybody that I've placed in a nursing home to return home. They are there for a reason, and usually family can't maintain the level of care and community resources are limited.

I decide that the dogs can't stay at work so I walk them back to the apartment. Bella and Sergeant have had enough excitement and will probably sleep all day. I hope that the dogs and Sophie don't trash the house. Sophie loves to play with the toilet paper, Sergeant collects my shoes, and Bella loves snooping in the bathroom trash can.

I decide to drive my blue Honda Civic, as I want to listen to my Rolling Stones CD, *Get Yer Ya-Ya's Out*. The drive will take about one half hour. I'll drop by the agency and Sally-Sue can drive the county car to Newport News.

The drive is just what the doctor's ordered. I have the song, *Midnight Rambler* blasting and I'm singing along.

Did you hear about the Midnight Rambler?
He'll leave his footsteps up and down your hall

138

WIND CHIMES   Teresa Adele Bettino

Did you hear about the Midnight Rambler?
Did you see me make my midnight call?

I stop singing. The person that broke into my apartment came just after midnight. I wonder who the Midnight Rambler is. I have my suspicions. I saw a parked Dodge Ram and somebody limping up the street.

Well, it's time to meet with Sally-Sue so I park my car and enter the bricked two-story office building. I tell myself to look happy as I enter the office. I visit a few minutes with two child protective service workers, Charlene and Meredith. Sally-Sue's in her office and waves as she sees me. I enter. She looks frazzled.

"Francie, I just had the keys in my hand. Can you bend down and look under my desk."

I'm not your wench.

Her office, although neat, has a pile of files on the floor.

"No keys under your desk, Sally-Sue."

She reaches into the pockets of her jacket and locates the car keys. We leave the building and walk to the parking lot, not speaking. The county car, a white Chevrolet has not been cleaned in months, and when we open the doors, the odor of McDonald's hamburgers is present along with the odor of stale greasy French fries. Two

McDonald's bags have been tossed onto the back seat.

Sally-Sue: "A bunch of slobs work for this department."

Sally-Sue starts the engine. The car needs gas.

"Sally-Sue, I think that we're in need of filling the tank. You know the new rule about the tank always on one half and above."

It's amazing to me that workers don't give a damn about the next poor schmuck taking the county car out. Workers smoke, drink liquor and have had sex in these cars. I once opened a county car trunk and found a discarded Trojan wrapper. Nice touch.

Sally-Sue drives to the county gas station and can't remember which side of the car that the tank's on.

"It's on the other side."

"Are you sure?"

"Yep."

Instead of going around and correcting this, Sally-Sue does the ultimate short cut. She maneuvers the car and opens her car door, leaning out to see if she can angle the vehicle and get closer to the pump. It doesn't work. She gasses the car in reverse, we lurch, and Sally-Sue falls out of the car. The car moves backwards. I lean over, grab the wheel and place my left foot

140

on the brake. The car stops. I turn it off and bolt out of the passenger side.

Sally-Sue's sitting up with a dazed look and motor oil is all over her. Her linen suit is tattered and blackish in color. Sally-Sue's hands and knees are bleeding. So much for "dressing for success" as Juney Bea preaches.

As I catch a closer look, I see that Sally-Sue's pants have split. She's wearing bright purple thong underwear. Sally-Sue has just given a new meaning to the word, "Mooning." Even though it's pretty gross to see Sally-Sue in this position, I don't want to miss this opportunity. I quickly grab my cell, and start videotaping. This will look good on YouTube. I'll have to figure out who I can send it to so that it can't be traced to me. She's too dazed to suspect what I'm doing. Mom and Jodi will love this. The ultimate, Sally-Sue Moon!

I help Sally-Sue into the back seat of the Chevy brushing French fries and hamburger crumbs onto the floor and we're off to Patient First. No meeting today about "No Back Door". Sally-Sue's treated for abrasions and given a blanket to cover her ass. I return Ms. Moon to the back door of Social Services and park the car.

I get into my Honda; crank-up the Stones and head back to Chincoteague. I'll have to watch the video of Sally-Sue with a glass of wine and a

141

joint later in the evening.   I'm listening to *Sympathy for the Devil* as my cell phone rings.

"Hi, partner in crime."

"Hi, Jodi, how are you, what's up?"

"Well, I want to report a vagrant whose just turned 60, living in a boxed house at the southern portion of the island by the marina."

"What? You can't be serious. It's not against the law to be homeless and if he's competent Jodi, I'm not going to deal with this."

"I need a favor. When are you going to be back in Chincoteague?"

"In about 40 minutes."

"I'll meet you there."

"OK. Good-bye."

My mind is on overdrive as I ride back to Chincoteague. Does this vagrant have anything to do with the murders? I change the channel back to *Midnight Rambler* as I drive north on Route 13.

13

The few hours spent at the precinct getting interrogated by Investigator Walsh and Burgess was a bunch of shit. Although Lou didn't mind the bad cop, good cop roles as he enjoyed being questioned by Investigator Burgess. What a cutie she is with blonde hair, blue eyes and a set of knockers. Lou smiles thinking of Investigator Burgess. He was released after three hours. Not bad. They have nothing on me.

Lou walks. His voices are talking to each other. He decides not to go directly home as he feels certain that he's being followed. He puts out his thumb and gets picked up by some guy dressed in black driving a Dodge Ram.

Once returned to Chincoteague, I decide to go out on the adult report that I received on Tuesday. I locate the report under mounds of paper and review it. This should be a slam dunk. The client, Margo Newman, lives on the main land in a section called Helltown, also known as Modest Town. There used to be a boarding home in this place. Ms. Newman is probably like the rest of my caseload, an old lady who doesn't have family to check-up on her, and she's probably a hoarder, too.

After searching real estate and establishing who owns this home, I look up Ms. Newman's amount of social security received, which is $500. Not much to live on. I print a Benefit Application so that she can apply for Medicaid and food stamps and grab a screening form so that I can assess her functioning. Prior to leaving, I snatch a piece of chocolate for stamina, the keys to the county car, a bottle of water, then leave.

I plug in my GPS system, as I don't have the time to get lost. The place is located about four miles from Zion Church. I pick out her house the moment that I'm driving down the road that she lives on. I almost have a sixth sense about clients' homes. The small rundown house is a "saltbox" looking as though it's been here since the 1700's. I pull up and open the door to the county car looking around just in case there's a loose dog or two. No barking, which is a good sign. I decide to keep the car door open just in case I need to make a mad dash from the front porch. I spot an old hound on the front porch. Poor thing looks pitiful. He's thin, dirty and mangy.

"Hi, puppy. Don't let me disturb you." I say as I reach to knock on the front door.

144

"Hello, is anyone home? Ms. Newman, this is Social Services, please come to your door."

No answer. I decide to take a walk around the house. Maybe the old lady's in the kitchen. I climb the back porch steps and my right foot falls through the rotten top step. The porch is decayed with trash all over the porch. Not just one or two plastic bags, mounds of it, some not in plastic bags, some in buckets. I step over a mound and make my way to the back door. I peer inside looking through a soiled lace curtain. Ms. Newman's sitting at her kitchen table.

I knock and see Ms. Newman looking over.

"Ms. Newman, I'm Francie Batista with social services." I try the knob. Locked.

"Please come to the door as I need to speak with you."

I watch Ms. Newman strain to get up from the table and see her grabbing for her cane. She's frail and looks like she is going to fall over. She comes to the door and opens it.

"Hi! Are you Ms. Newman?"

Ms. Newman shakes her head up and down.

"I'm Francie Batista a social worker and am here to check up on you. Someone called and said that you've been falling a lot. Is that so? Can I come in and talk with you?"

Ms. Newman opens the door wider and I take a whiff. The stench is overpowering, as it's a combination of rotten food and shit.

145

"Come here and sit down at the table, dear."

There's no way that I'm going to put my butt on anything in this home. What did they teach us in Social Work 101? I wished I'd listened. I think I need to find something wooden, without fabric.

"Ms. Newman thanks for asking me to sit, but I have been sitting at my desk all day. I think if you don't mind, that I will stand for a minute. I feel as though I need to stretch. Tell me, how are you doing?"

"What did you say? You need to speak up. I'm hard of hearing."

"Ms. Newman thanks for asking me to sit, but I have been sitting at my desk all day. I think if you don't mind, that I will stand for a minute. I feel as though I need to stretch. Tell me, how are you doing?" I reply with my voice cracking.

"Well, I'm turning 88 in a few weeks."

"What is your date of birth?"

"I was born in July, 1952."

"It says on the report that you were born on October 12, 1920. Do you know what month this is?"

"Yes, it's December."

My pager suddenly goes off. It's Sally-Sue Moon.

"Ms. Newman. My pager has gone off and I need to call my supervisor. I will be right back."

146

She nods. Somehow, I don't think that she made this connection. I leave out the back door, climb over a mound of trash and make my way to the county car. I speed dial Sally-Sue.

"Hi, Sally-Sue, did you just page me?"

"No. I paged Wanda Burton."

"Sally-Sue, my pager went off and it has your phone number on it."

"Well, I don't know how your pager got my number. I paged Wanda Burton."

"Yeah, right, OK, I'm interviewing an elderly lady who self-neglects. By the way, Sally-Sue, I haven't seen Wanda in a couple of days. Has she taken some time off?"

"I think so. I have to go, bye." Sally-Sue states as she hangs up the phone abruptly.

I close the door to the car. The wind is blowing and I hear wind chimes. I look and see about ten horse chimes hanging from an old oak tree. I walk over to the tree. All the chimes are moving to the rhythm of the breeze, with pleasant melodies. I see some chains without chimes. Suddenly it hits me.

Oh my God!

I speed dial Jodi, and Jodi answers, first ring.

"It's me Jodi, and you're not going to believe this. I'm over in Helltown interviewing Ms. Newman and she has a bunch of horse wind chimes in her oak tree." She lives in a "saltbox" near the church."

"I'm on my way."

The dog's still sleeping soundly on the front porch and I decide to walk to the back door. I skip a couple of steps for fear of falling through and climb again over trash. I find Ms. Newman exactly where I left her.

"Ms. Newman, do you have any adult children?"

"What'd you say, dear? I can't hear you."

Jodi arrives in about twenty minutes. I hear her car and proceed to walk from the kitchen through the dining room to the living room. There's a path. Ms. Newman's definitely a hoarder. I open the front door. The good old hound remains in the same place peacefully sleeping. Jodi's counting missing wind chimes. Five chimes are missing from chains. Jodi comes to the porch. We walk into the front of the house being careful not to wake Cujo.

"Ms. Newman, I have Investigator Jodi Burgess with me. She would like to ask you a few questions."

"What did you say, dear?"

"Ms. Newman, I'm Investigator Jodi Burgess with Chincoteague Sheriff's Department. Francie called me to come over to your place to speak with you. Are you able to hear me?"

"I hear you just fine."

"I'm interested in your wind chimes. Can you tell me where you got those?"

148

"The wind chimes did you say?"

"Yes, Ms. Newman, the chimes."

"Oh. What do you want to know?"

I feel like taking my hands, placing them around this old lady's neck, and shaking her until she spills the beans. Patience is a virtue.

"Ms. Newman, you have horse wind chimes hanging from the oak tree in front of the house. Can you tell me about why you have these?"

"Honey, I've had chimes for years. Momma collected them. Her momma too. Always the same."

"Why?"

"What, did you say?"

"Ms. Newman, I am trying to understand why your momma had so many wind chimes."

"I can tell that you're not from these parts, honey."

"Can you explain?"

"My momma was born, raised and died here. Her momma was born, raised and died here. Folk lore, legend, myth whatever you want to call it weighs heavy in this neck of the Eastern Shore."

"Yes, I understand."

"So you want me to tell you about the chimes?"

"We would love to hear about this folk lore."

"Momma believed that when somebody passed, that their soul needed something to attach itself to. Chincoteague ponies are wild and free. They serve as portals. When the first breeze moves the chimes, which is attached to the person upon their death, their soul attaches itself to the chime. The wild spirit of the Chincoteague pony carries the deceased soul to the next world. Country folk believe in the spirit of these wild ponies. There's only a handful of us left that believe in this legend.

Jodi and I glance across the room at each other. A chill runs up my spine, the third in a couple of days. I'm wondering who this lady knows or doesn't as somebody has been ripping off wind chimes. Of course, we know that she's not the killer. She can't even walk across the room without falling.

"Ms. Newman, do you have kin living in this area?"

"What?"

"Can you tell me the names of people that you call or visit you?"

"I've lost touch with them. Folks around here know about this folklore though. And kin of mine know. Somebody came by the other day and took some chimes, never asked just took. Momma would never have permitted that. Young folk have no manners today."

I walk over to her refrigerator and see a list of names. I take out a pad of paper and begin writing down names, addresses and phone numbers.   She has her doctor's name on the sheet, too.   I'll be busy calling and gleaning information for the next couple of days. Obviously, Ms. Newman needs some help.

"Ms. Newman I have to go, but I'll return. I'll put my card on your refrigerator.   Please have anybody coming to visit you give me a call. Thanks."

14

Jodi and I leave Ms. Newman sitting at the kitchen table. Jodi calls Chief Winston. It's two-thirty and Jodi needs to return to Chincoteague for a mandatory meeting. She says that she's going to call dispatch and request that a deputy stake out Margo Newman's place. The deputy pulling the shift will keep Jodi apprised. We say goodbye, and Jodi's hopeful that this killer will be caught as it's getting close to Wednesday. Her vacation starts Saturday.

As I'm driving back to the agency, I decide that Ms. Newman's risk has lowered significantly with this stake out. Maybe in a day or two I will have gathered information about her and can find somebody to take care of her. I'm hopeful that services can be set up so that she can be maintained at home. The house needs a good cleaning and a dumpster needs to be requested to get rid of all the clutter. I'll call the building inspector and we can coordinate and work as a team on this situation. Sally-Sue will approve of this service plan as she loves teamwork. It makes her look good as a supervisor.

My cell phone rings, and it's mom.

"Hi, Mom."

"Hi, Francie.   I'm on my way to Chincoteague as we speak. I should arrive in a couple of hours. The traffic near the tunnel is horrible."

"Mom, you really didn't have to come, but I'm glad you're coming. I really need to talk with you."

"I know, honey. See you soon."

I decide to swing by my apartment and get my stash of pot out of my place as mom's worse than a bloodhound. I park, run up the apartment steps and open the door. I see immediately that Sergeant and Bella have been busy as my slippers, yesterday's newspaper, and a roll of toilet paper litter my apartment. Sophie is nowhere to be seen.

I quickly clean up and get my stash, placing it at the bottom of a colorful Biscotti jar. On top of the pot, I fill the jar with Twinkies.

I decide to take Sergeant and Bella to work with me.   They're ready to get out of this small apartment.   Bella runs ahead of Sergeant and once outside, the two run circles around me, begging for attention. I let them run for a few minutes and both get tired and come to me. I open the back door of the county car and they climb in. I place the Biscotti jar in the trunk.

I pull up to the agency and park in the lot behind the library. It's a small park and my dogs love it. I have a tennis ball and I throw it for the dogs to chase. Bella isn't interested. She's excited about all the ducks hanging around, but Sergeant retrieves the ball. He's a natural. Sergeant returns the ball and I throw it again and again. Bella's content to sniff around. After a few more throws, I stop, walk to the car and open the trunk. The Biscotti jar's still as pretty as ever and remains in one piece. I carry it to the back door of the agency, open the door, and the dogs run in happy to be returning to work.

I walk through the kitchen, down the small hallway to the reception area. Wanda's   not there. Phone messages are blinking on her telephone. Since she's not at work I place the Biscotti jar on her desk. The dogs follow me to the front door. I make them sit and stay as I flip the sign to open on the door.
"Good dogs. Let's go to the back, I've got work to do."

Lou's voices are tongue-tied. He's thinking that his luck is running out. He should have his Glock with him. First, getting interrogated by deputies and now, getting into this old truck with this crazed looking dude. The guy appears high on something, not pot. His eyes have darkness to them like he's getting ready to kill somebody.

This look is familiar to Lou. Guys in Nam had this look before going on a shooting spree. Lou's voices are telling him to get off at the next stop.

"Hey, can you let me out on Seaside Road?"

Without a word, this guy pulls over and stops the truck. He looks over to Lou. His eyes remain dark.

"Thanks, man. I appreciate the ride."

Lou gets out and starts walking. The guy floors his pick-up and sends gravel flying onto Lou, hitting him in the back of the head. *What an asshole.*

Lou begins his walk. He's on his way to visit his aunt who he hasn't seen in twenty years. She lives in Modest Town in a small spot that used to be called Helltown. She's probably close to ninety by now, if she's still living.

Jodi and Andy arrive at headquarters for a mandatory meeting. Ben Benson's speaking to Chief Winston. The meeting starts promptly.

Ben Benson: "We have some leads that have developed. Trooper Goode, profiler for the department is going to catch everybody up."

"I'd like to thank you for working hard and giving up your spare time so that this killer can be brought to justice. First of all, there are two killers. The murders of Tony Smith, recently identified by family, he's the elderly guy that

155

was found in Muddy Creek; Maureen Hughes, the federal park ranger; Michael Surry, the gentleman found murdered in Cape Charles; Sally and Ned Melton of Chincoteague and the horse, Star, were shot with the same murder weapon. The weapon's a 40-Glock. The Chincoteague pony was shot with a 40-Glock, but it's not the same weapon. I have nothing else to report. I will answer any questions that you might have."

A deputy in the middle row has his hand raised. "So what you're saying is that we have a copy-cat killer?"

"What I'm saying is that we have two killers. The person who killed the pony didn't leave a wind chime. I don't think he's a copycat."

Investigator Burgess, I see your hand raised.

"I've just returned from the home of Margo Newman. She lives in Modest Town, Helltown, whatever, and hanging from her oak tree are horse wind chimes. The sheriff's department from Nelsonia is staking out the house and property. There are some chains hanging from the tree without any chimes. My count is five, exactly the number of those murdered by one of the killers."

Ben Benson: "With this new information, hopefully the killer will return and we can nail him. I would like to commend everybody for working hard. We are close. Let's continue to

156

keep our eyes and ears open. Hopefully by
tomorrow this time we will have caught the
bastards. I'll turn the rest of the meeting over to
the captain. Thanks."

Chief Winston ends the meeting by spitting
some snuff into a Coke can. As Jodi is leaving,
he walks up to her.

"Good job, Jodi."

"Thanks, Chief."

Jodi leaves the meeting. She wants Francie to
interview Lou Mann. Jodi feels that Francie can
get information from him as social workers are
known for their caring and compassion for
mankind. Obviously, if Lou is living in a box,
he's in need of help.

It's vital that we get these killers soon, before
another person turns up shot between the eyes or
another horse is executed. She looks down at her
yellow diamond ring. Key West is a few days
away. As Jodi starts down the front steps of the
precinct, Andy's waiting for her.

"What's our next step?"

"To get Francie to interview Lou Mann with
me listening in on the conversation."

"Do you need any help?"

"No, Andy, you go home and get some sleep."

"Thanks, partner."

As Jodi continues walking to her car she feels
some cooler air coming onto the island. Jodi

157

looks at the flower bed along the sidewalk. A lone duck is standing with one leg tucked under his feathers. He looks as though he's gotten into a fight. *I hope someone didn't try and hurt this little one. If he's still there in a couple of hours, I'll call animal control.*

Jodi drives to the agency. She parks in the back and uses the back door. Just as she's about to enter, Jodi looks to her left. The new bridge is getting further along. *I wonder how much longer it will be until this bridge is completely finished?* Jodi opens the back door, goes through the kitchen and finds Francie in her office.

Francie's at the fax machine when Jodi comes through the front door.

"Hey what's up?"

"I thought that if you had a moment, I'd like for you to interview Lou Mann. He's the drifter I spoke with you about earlier today and he's still a suspect."

"Why do you want me to interview him?"

"I think that he will open up to you as you're a social worker. Social workers are helpful and sympathetic. I don't think that Lou saw us in that light."

"I don't know, Jodi. You know that I would love to help, but you know that if he wants to be homeless and live in a house box, he has the right to self-determination."

"Come on. Please? I'll buy you a coffee. I see that Wanda has some Biscottis. They are good with Cappuccino."

"Um…I'll skip the Biscotti and take you up on the Cappuccino. Can we take Bella and Sergeant? They wrecked my apartment and I don't want them to tear up my office."

We take the dogs down to Sundial Books and visit with Jon and Jane for a few minutes. I order a Cappuccino.

Jodi drives to the southern tip of the island. Lou has set up housekeeping across from Curtis Merritt Harbor. Everybody gets out of the car. The dogs run ahead. They are chasing sea gulls, air and sand.

Lou's makeshift house is easily located, as a small well-beaten path has emerged between two dunes. Lou has found a million dollar location. He's staked his living quarters well, hidden from normal traffic with a magnificent view of Chincoteague Channel.

"Wow. This is really neat, Jodi. I don't think that he's home though. He would have greeted us. I peek in, and I see a sleeping bag, some clothes and books. Do you want me to crawl in and nose around while you keep watch?"

"I don't have a warrant to search his stuff."

"I don't need one. You look out as I don't want him to know that I'm doing this."

I crawl in. The books he reads are fiction. James Patterson, Dean Koontz, and John Grisham. I crawl back a little further and find a flashlight, matches, soap and deodorant.

"Francie, come on out. We need to leave. How about if you leave your card and then he can contact you?"

I leave my professional card attached to the inside of one of Lou Mann's sneakers.

We retrieve the dogs and Jodi drives me back to the agency. I get out with the dogs in front of the agency on Main Street. Sergeant spots Jon outside of the book store and runs down the sidewalk to greet him. Bella, my protector, stays back. Jon returns Sergeant after a few minutes. He's out of breath as Jon has treated him to a tennis ball. He's been throwing the ball to him at the small park behind the agency.

"Jon have you seen Wanda anytime while I've been gone?"

"No. There have been a few islanders waiting for the agency to open while you have been out. But no Wanda."

"I could really use somebody, anybody to help around here. I need another body, Jon. Without Wanda, the office is open sporadically. I asked my supervisor, Sally-Sue Moon for some help and she said, "No." Jon would you like to see what Sally-Sue looks like?

I remove my cell phone from my pocketbook and put the video on.

"That's your supervisor?"

"Yup. She fell out of the county car. I never knew that she wore thong underwear."

"Nice purple thongs. Did she get hurt?

"A little, I wished for more though."

"Francie, you have a mean streak in you."

"I know and I don't care. You should have her as your supervisor."

"Hey Francie, I like the Biscotti jar on Wanda's desk. Nice touch. I don't recall seeing it on her desk the last time I was here."

"Oh. Wanda just acquired it."

"That would look good in my café. Maybe I could pay her for it."

"Possibly. You'll have to ask her when she returns to work."

Jon leaves through the front door.

I think that I need to move that Biscotti jar as it's drawing a lot of attention. Who knew that everybody loves Biscotti and the colorful jar to boot! Go figure.

15

Wanda's in bed with her significant other, Jeanna. Jeanna works for the post office as a clerk. They've been an item for about three months. She hears a knock on her apartment door.

"Who the hell can that be?" and Wanda walks over to the door and peeps.

"You've got to be kidding." Wanda says as she sees her mother standing there staring into the hole.

"Jeanna, you better get up and dressed. It's my mother."

"What the heck is she doing here?"

"I don't know, but I'll guess that it has something to do with my not going to work all week."

Jeanna springs from the bed, pulls her jeans over her hips and throws a T-shirt over her head, onto her shoulders and stomach. She goes into the bathroom to wash her face and give her teeth a quick brushing.

Wanda opens the door. Pat enters with an overnight bag.

"Hi, mom. What's going on?"

"You can probably figure out what's going on. I'll give you three tries."

"OK...so I haven't been at work. I needed some space from Francie Batista and those worthless sacks called clients."

"Sally-Sue and Juney Bea want you back at work today or else you're going to lose your job. Don't even think that I'm going to support you and your habits."

Jeanna opens the door to the bathroom and walks into the living room.

"Um...mom this is my friend, Jeanna. She was just visiting and needs to go to work."

"It's my pleasure to meet you, Ms. Burton." Jeanna, behind Pat's back, holds her hand to her ear indicating to Wanda to call her later. Wanda shakes her head yes.

"Wanda, what in God's name is going on? Are you taking your medications? You know, I don't need this shit."

Gertrude Batista arrives in Chincoteague and drives directly to the agency. She opens the agency door. Two dogs come to greet her. Francie is following closely. She sees her mother, quickens her pace and gives her mom a big hug.

"Mom, it's so good to see you. I really need you. A Chincoteague pony has been murdered and I'm really scared. No one knows who came into my apartment. I think that this murderer is after me."

"I know, honey. That's why I'm here. Has Wanda been at work yet this week?"

"Nope. When I mentioned it to Sally-Sue, she blew me off."

"How about if I spend some time going through Wanda's desk?"

"OK. But don't move too much around, just in case Wanda returns. She will know if somebody's been snooping."

Gertrude walks into Wanda's space and proceeds to open the center drawer of Wanda's desk. Wanda has a bunch of junk in her center drawer. Pencils; rubber bands; paper clips; yellow sticky notes and a few cards from friends, one of which is from her mother, Pat Burton. She opens the card from Pat. The card is designed from an animal rescue foundation, Save a Life Animal Rescue. One of the dog's eyes has been etched out and somebody has sketched a hangman's noose around the dog's neck.

Gertrude reads the card. She'll reread it later and stuffs the card inside of her back jean pocket. Somebody's at the front door.

Jodi Burgess enters and smiles when she sees Gertrude.

"Hi, Gertrude. How are you?"

"I'm fine. I wish that I were visiting under a different circumstance. I hear that you're going on vacation to Key West."

"If we don't catch this murderer or murderers, I won't be doing anything. The chief has suspended all leave. I think that we're getting closer to motive and person. Is Francie around? I need to ask her if she would like to go to Key West with me. My college friend has H1N1."

Jodi enters Francie's office and finds her on the floor separating sections of a foster care record. "Do you believe all the documents and papers in this teenager's case record? There's even a copy of a birthday card."

"Have you heard from Lou Mann?"

"Nope, not yet. Maybe he hasn't returned so far."

"I wonder where he is. He hasn't been spotted walking around on the island."

"Maybe I need to drive back to his place?"
"Let's just see what happens. Oh Francie, Elaine, my college buddy that was going to come to Key West with me can't, she has H1N1 and is in bed too contagious to travel. I was wondering if you would like to come? Everything's paid for."

"I'd love to go for the week. I'll send Sally-Sue an e-mail and ask mom if she would watch the critters."

"Just remember that I can't go until these murderers are found."

"What do you mean murderers?"

"The gun that killed the Chincoteague pony was from a different gun. Trooper Goode thinks that it was not the chime killer."

"Oh great, two lunatics walking around. Does my mom know this?"

"No, I didn't tell her. You can explain, as I need to get going. Thanks for agreeing to go with me, Francie. I really didn't want to go by myself."

"No problem. I've not been to the Florida Keys so this should be really fun. The weather's usually hot and sunny there, just what I like."

"Jodi, I have something to show you on my cell phone. You need to guess who this is."

With my cell phone on video, I hand the phone to Jodi. She instantly starts laughing and takes a seat at my desk.

Bart Connors decides to visit with his aunt. He uses his GPS system, as he gets confused once away from Chincoteague Island and Watts Estates. He remembers family visits to see Aunt Margo as a child and loved hearing Aunt Margo speak of the legend of the wind chimes hanging from the branches on her oak tree. Bart's father, George, believed in this myth.

166

From Watts Estates it takes about thirty minutes to get to the shack. As he's looking for the house, he sees somebody going up the front steps. He also spots a car parked a little bit up the street and wonders what's up. He decides that he better drive by and will return when the person and the car aren't there. Bart proceeds to Chincoteague, as he needs to pick up something that he left near the marina.

Lou's hitched another ride and is let off in front of his aunt's house. It looks like a shack. Certainly not how he remembers the place. The oak tree still has wind chimes. He walks up to the front porch. Garbage, clutter and an old hound dog are fixtures. He knocks, doesn't get a reply and walks around to the back of the house. The steps are rotten like everything else around here. He peers in the windowed back door and looks through a dirty lace curtain. He sees a figure lying in a fetal position on the floor. Lou jiggles the door handle; it's not locked and he walks in.
Standing over his aunt he notices how dirty and cluttered the kitchen is. It smells of rotten eggs, urine and feces.
    "Aunt Margie, it is Lou."
Lou helps Margo Newman up from the floor. She stinks of urine and crap. Aunt Margie's unkempt, disheveled and her hair is matted. She

167

certainly doesn't look like the aunt that he remembers.

"Aunt Margie, I came to visit with you. I've been staying in Chincoteague and thought that I would come by and say hi. How about if I make you something to eat? How long have you been on the floor?"

"What? Who are you?"

The front door opens and Sally-Sue Moon comes briskly in, obviously in a hurry. She appears startled when she recognizes Gertrude. Sergeant and Bella come from Francie's office to greet her. Gertrude and Sally-Sue never cared for one another, not even during college days and with the passing of years, with both working in the social work profession, their animosity grew.

"Hi Gertrude. What are you doing here?"

"I'm visiting my daughter. With all the murders and Wanda not showing for work, I thought that I would stay with her until the killer is apprehended."

"Where's Francie?"

"She's in the back. Investigator Jodi Burgess is speaking with her."

Sally-Sue walks to the back of the agency.

Jodi hears that it's Sally-Sue and puts the cell phone in her pocket. She gets up from Francie's desk chair.

"Oh, Jodi. I heard that you were back here with Francie. How are you doing?"

"Stressed."

Francie turns and faces her supervisor. "Hi, Sally-Sue. How are you feeling? Have your hands and knees healed from your fall?"

"Yes. Thanks for asking. Has Wanda come to work today?"

"I haven't seen her."

"I'm going to look inside of her desk. There's something there that I need."

Sally-Sue goes to Wanda's desk. Gertrude takes the hint and leaves to go get some air. She decides to walk over to the Mall.

Sally-Sue rummages through Wanda's desk. She reads a couple cards. One in particular catches her eye as it's signed, "I love you, Jeanna." *Great day in the morning, the girl's a lesbian.*

Sally-Sue comes across the Biscotti jar sitting on Wanda's desk. She decides to take it. Her cat, Scruffy, knocked over her Biscotti jar and broke it into pieces a few weeks ago. It had been displayed on the kitchen counter and that cat, which has been nothing but trouble, shouldn't have been climbing on the kitchen counter. Sally-Sue smiles as she holds the Biscotti jar. It has vibrant colors matching the colors of her kitchen wallpaper.

169

"Francie, I'm taking Wanda's Biscotti jar. Tell her to give me a call when she gets in to work. Oh, and get rid of your dogs. It's inappropriate to have them at the agency."

"Are you sure about the jar? I mean, it is Wanda's."

"Yeah, I gave it to her recently and want it back."

Indian giver. Liar, Liar, your purple thongs are on fire.

Gertrude comes out of the Mall and sees Sally-Sue leaving. *What a snake! I wonder what she's up to? What's Sally-Sue doing with Wanda's Biscotti jar?* She enters the agency.

Gertrude takes the greeting card out of her pocket.

"Francie and Jodi, look what I've found in Wanda's desk drawer."

Jodi: "Gertrude, since I don't have a search warrant, I don't want to touch it. Do you think that this is evidence?"

"Yes. I really think that this is something to look into. Look at the eye and neck of this dog on the front of this card. Didn't you say that two horses had been murdered?

170

WIND CHIMES   Teresa Adele Bettino

Dear Wanda,

I have spoken with Sally-Sue about your application. You really need this job as this is a perfect opportunity for you to change your life. I will not continue to support you. This is your golden opportunity. Juney Bea has agreed for you to be hired. All you need to do, honey, is to show up for the interview.

Love,
Mom

P.S. When you get to Chincoteague, please check up on your great-aunt, Margie, from time to time. If you don't remember where she lives, give me a call. Thanks, sweetie.

171

16

Pat and her daughter stare at one another not sure as to what to say. There's a large wedge between mother and daughter. Pat can't understand her daughter, as she can't figure out what goes on in Wanda's head. She's always been a difficult moody type even as a child she was a loner.

"And who's this Jeanna?"

"Who do you think she is?"

"I really don't know, but have some idea."

"Well, Mom, I'm a lesbian. I came out of the closet in high school only you were looking the other way."

"How about if we change the subject? Why do you think that I'm here, Wanda?"

"Let me guess, Sally-Sue called and told you that I haven't been at work for the past three days."

"What the hell is going on with you?"

"I needed some time off. Frankly, I'm sick of this place and hate my job."

"That doesn't mean that you don't show up for work. You have job responsibilities."

"Mom, I don't give a rat's ass."

"What's the noise I hear in the back bedroom?"

"Oh, I got a Chihuahua from Chincoteague Rescue."

"Wanda, you can't keep the dog. You know your history. I won't let you mutilate that dog."

Wanda grabs her backpack and brushes into her mother's side, causing Pat to fall onto a chair. She slams the door and the scenic picture of beach and Chincoteague ponies falls off of the wall. Pat hears the Dodge leaving and the dog crying.

Pat is shaking. Her nerves are on edge. She's afraid to open the back bedroom door for fear of what she may find. She hears the dog whimpering as she gets nearer to the door. She cautiously opens the door. The dog has been chained to the leg of the bed. It has cross marks, linear in design across its back. There's no food or water. The dog has gone to the bathroom. Feces and urine permeate the air, and Pat gags. The dog, so small and delicate is shaking, and there's a crust of blood around the dog's right eye.

Pat starts crying and takes the dog off of the chain and hugs her. At this moment Pat realizes how mentally ill Wanda is. *How can this be? She has been given every opportunity. God knows I've given and done everything in my*

173

power and nothing obviously has worked. My
God, my daughter's Satan.
Pat kisses the dog, and finds some shampoo and
places the dog in the kitchen sink. She tenderly
washes her and cleans her wounds. Pat dries the
little one with a bathroom towel, locates another
towel and wraps the dog. She carries the dog out
of the apartment and to her car. Pat needs to
purchase some food and to locate a vet. Wanda
needs to be held accountable for her actions.
This abusive behavior can't be ignored.

James Parker drives to Watts Estates. He has
Elizabeth on his mind. He enters the barn and
sees Elizabeth mucking stalls. She hears
footsteps and turns. Princess, her Corgi, growls
at James. He approaches hurriedly. James is in
one of his dark moods. Elizabeth knows him
well. His clothing is disheveled, hair slicked
back and he's thrashing his cane as he limps up
to her.
Elizabeth doesn't wait to find out what his
problem is. She knows his dark side and isn't
going to be a victim. Elizabeth throws a pitch
fork at him and runs out the back door of the
barn.
She runs to Bart Connors' farm. He's not there.
She sees him pulling up in his truck and runs to
him. Bart's always ready for action and has a
license to carry a gun. It's registered and he has

it inside of his truck. Bart takes his Glock out of the hoister, checks the magazine, racks the slide and puts one in the chamber. He's got plenty of rounds. He knows that it's James. He's a nobody, useless.

Bart methodically advances towards Elizabeth's barn. He loves the adrenaline rush. Perfect, on this warm fall night and with a full moon to add atmosphere for killing.

He's near to the barn and sees James.

That prick Bart Connors is out to get him. James scrambles into his pick-up as he sees Bart approaching the barn. James as he's leaving shoots Bart the finger and points his Glock in Bart's direction. Bart turns around and runs back home rushing to get into his truck to follow James.

Elizabeth looks out of Bart's barn and sees both men leaving. She decides to return home with Princess, lock her door and sleep with her revolver.

Sally-Sue's driving the county car back to the main agency in Accomack. She's just driven over the bridge and is nearing Wallops Island. Sally-Sue sees a roadblock and stops.

An officer approaches the car with a German Shepherd at his side. "License and registration, ma'am."

"I don't know if the registration is in this car as it's not my vehicle, it belongs to the government."

"Well, government cars need to be registered."

"OK officer, I'll look."

The dog starts sniffing the night air. Its head is up and the officer looks at the dog. He walks the dog over to the trunk. The dog's sniffing the trunk and barking. He sits stoically.

"Ma'am, please get out of the car. Take your key out of the ignition and walk to the trunk area."

Sally-Sue complies.

"Is there anything in this trunk that you are aware of that would make my dog act like this, um...Ms. Moon?"

"No sir. I just placed a Biscotti jar in the trunk, officer."

Sally-Sue opens the trunk and hands the Biscotti jar to the officer. The dog goes nuts. The officer opens the lid, takes out a handful of Twinkies and feels a plastic bag. He slowly brings the bag out of the jar, looks at it, recognizes that the plastic bag contains marijuana and calls for backup.

Investigator Jodi Burgess hears the call over her radio. "Francie and Gertrude I have to go. Something's happened near Wallops. Francie, call me on my cell if Lou comes by."

"Oh, here's your cell back. Good video of Sally-Sue's purple thongs."

"I thought you would like the view."

Lou cooks his aunt a scrambled egg and makes her some coffee. The stuff in the refrigerator is outdated and moldy. His aunt obviously needs somebody to take care of her. Aunt Margie's eating as if she hasn't eaten in weeks and she probably hasn't.

Lou hears a vehicle pull up in the front yard. The dog starts to bark. He walks through the dining room area, into the living room and trips on a pile of newspapers. Lou peers from the front window. A person driving a truck is in the driveway.

Deputy Walt Pearson, a deputy from Nelsonia, puts in a call to Investigator Jodi Burgess.

"I've got two people visiting Margo Newman. One's inside and the other's sitting in the driveway. Do you want me to approach?"

"No. I'm not far from you."

Jodi finds Sally-Sue on the side of the road in front of Wallops Island. State police, county police and military have surrounded her county vehicle. Jodi sees Ben Benson in the crowd.

"Ben, what's going on?   Sally-Sue's a supervisor of the Department of Social Services."

"Well, she may be a supervisor, but she's a pot-head. She was transporting marijuana in a Biscotti jar. The officer also found a perfume bottle of Patchouli oil. Didn't those Hippies in the sixties use the stuff to mask the odor of pot?"

"Yeah, I think so."

"She's gotten her one call and contacted the Director of Social Services, Juney Bea Karring. Ms. Karring is on her way. Sally-Sue will be spending the night in the Accomack Regional Jail. Tomorrow she can explain her story to the judge. She claims that the stash isn't hers, that she took the Biscotti jar off of Wanda Burton's desk, who is an eligibility worker.

"Ben, since this is tied up I have something going on at Modest Town. I've had it staked out and two people have shown up. This old lady has horse wind chimes hanging on her oak tree. How about coming with me?"

"I wouldn't miss this for the world."

Lou opens the front door of his aunt's shack. The old hound runs in baying. Lou goes out onto the front porch.

Deputy Pearson watches.

"Who the hell are you, standing in my aunt's driveway?"

178

"Who the hell are you?"

"It's none of your fucking business."

The female turns quickly and jumps inside her truck headed towards Route 679.

Lou goes back into the house to the kitchen. The dog's half starved and has its front paws on the kitchen table eating scramble eggs.

"Aunt Margie, what the hell's going on here?"

James is manic. He's driving around pissed at Elizabeth and seeking vengeance on Bart. He wants to level Bart Connors. He's near Wallops Island when he sees a roadblock, flashing blue lights and all these cops. A county car is surrounded. He goes down a side street. James drives down Route 679 and sees a truck speeding in the other direction. He looks in his rear view mirror and blue lights are flashing.

Ben Benson and Investigator Burgess have pulled him over.

"License and registration."

"What's the problem?"

"Step out of your vehicle, sir."

James Parker gets out of his truck and Jodi recognizes him immediately.

"James, where are you headed?"

"I'm just driving around. Elizabeth and I aren't getting along. We've had a fight and I'm blowing off steam."

"It looks like you circumvented the road block."

"I did what?"

"You saw the road block and turned down a side street."

"What's going on with the road block? I've never known of a road block in front of Wallops Island."

"You didn't answer my question."

Ben Benson: "Step to the side, turn and face your vehicle, hands on the roof of the vehicle and legs apart."

James gets out of the vehicle. His gun is sitting on the passenger's seat, clearly visible." Ben spots it immediately. He nods to Jodi. She sees the gun.

Ben calls for back up. There is enough probable cause to cover their asses with this arrest. He has a Glock sitting in the front passenger's seat. This is sufficient reason to arrest this asshole. He's probably the wind chime killer.

Jodi calls for back up. They need to continue to Helltown to speak with whomever is visiting Margo Newman.

"James, you're being arrested."

Deputy Little arrives and reads James his rights. He's going to be off of the streets tonight and may not see the light of day for a very long time.

180

17

Lou leaves out the back door of his aunt's house. He walks behind her house through a neighbor's back yard. Lou decides to take another route back to Chincoteague. It's about five and he is hopeful that Francie Batista is still at work as he needs to speak with her about his aunt.

Lou doesn't feel good about leaving his aunt, however; he will return tomorrow. She's lived this long without his help and can live another day without him.

He's picked up by somebody driving a Honda Civic. As they pass Wallops Island both are rubber necking to see what's going on. It looks as though somebody in a county car is being arrested.

Lou returns to Chincoteague and gets dropped off near Pony Swim Lane. He walks back to his place in the dunes.

Somebody's ransacked his place. His voices aren't happy. They don't like all of this turmoil. Lou's food has been thrown all over his house box, his books are ripped to shreds and a stash of hash and what pot he had left has been taken.

Lou's concerned about the Glock. He walks over to the dune searching for the spot where he buried the gun. He digs. He feels the box, brings it out of the hole, opens it and the Glock is gone.

Somebody's dug it up and put the box back empty.

His voices are arguing amongst themselves. He holds his head. He kicks the ground and sand flies up hitting his eyes. He pulls down the zipper of his pants, takes a piss in the hole where the Glock was and decides to visit Francie Batista.

Wanda's had it. She's out for blood. Sally-Sue and Juney Bea need to be taught a lesson. She drives by the agency. Someone's sitting at her desk. She parks behind the agency. The library's cat is eating some food. She calls it over to her, however; it scampers. A duck waddles over for the cat's tidbits. Wanda remembers that she has a slingshot in the truck. She goes back to the truck, finds the slingshot, bends over and locates a rock. She slowly places the rock in the sling, breathes in, aims and hits the duck dead center. Feathers fly and the duck drops.

Lou reaches the front door of the agency. He walks up to the receptionist's desk and introduces himself. Gertrude notices urine stains

182

on his filthy pants. He smells of body odor. He requests to speak with Ms. Batista. Gertrude uses the phone's intercom.

"Francie, you have a gentleman named Lou Mann out here to speak with you."

"OK, mom, tell him to have a seat and I'll be right out."

Francie picks her cell phone up from the desk and speed dials Jodi.

"Jodi, where are you? Lou Mann's just walked in the front door and is sitting in the waiting area."

"I'm in front of Margo Newman's place. Two people came tonight, but it appears that we've lost them. I went in the house, spoke with Ms. Newman and nobody's here. I'm leaving now. Keep him there. I will come in through the back door."

"OK."

Pat's at a loss as to what to do. She's driving down Main Street and sees that the lights are on in the agency. Pat decides she's going to walk in and find out if there's a social worker available to speak with. She's fed the Chihuahua and she's sleeping peacefully, wrapped in a blanket that Pat purchased at the store. Her daughter needs help.

Jodi has her lights flashing and makes her way to Chincoteague in about fifteen minutes. Ben Benson is following her. He's pumped. Two killers and Lou Mann has to be the other one!

Wanda comes through the front door and sees Gertrude sitting at her desk.

"Who the hell are you sitting at my desk?"

"I'm Francie's mother. I assume by your voice tone that you're Wanda. I'm helping my daughter since you haven't shown up for work in almost five days."

"Well isn't that nice of you. You're a Pollyanna type just like your daughter. Now I know where she gets it from. I think that Francie said that you're a retired social worker. Well, imagine that."

Wanda eyes Lou Mann. He's sitting reading a *People* magazine.

"Who are you?"

"It's none of your business."

"How about, old man, that I make it my business?"

The front door opens and a woman enters holding a shaking Chihuahua.

"Mom, what the hell are you doing here?"

"I didn't know what to do. I came to speak with a social worker about you. You're sick and need help."

184

Jodi and Ben park in the back of the agency. Jodi sees the dead duck as she opens her car door. They draw their guns and come in through the kitchen.

"Mom, you really need to stay out of my life. I hate this job. You don't see that."

"I understand now, Wanda, that this job isn't for you. You need some more psychiatric help."

"What, because you found out that I'm a Lesbian today?   Is that what you're talking about?"

"No, I'm talking about what you did to this little precious dog. You need to be in treatment."

Francie walks into the reception area, with Sergeant and Bella following closely behind, pretending not to have heard this conversation.

"Hi, Wanda. How are you?"

"Go to hell, Hoe."

"Wanda, I don't understand why you hate me so much! Have I ever done anything to harm you?"

Lou stands up and pretends not to have heard the disrespect to Ms. Batista by this girl named Wanda.   He sees Francie surrounded by two large dogs and is a little apprehensive about the Pit-mix. He extends his right hand.

"You must be Francie Batista."

They shake hands as Francie nods yes.

"I need to speak with you about my aunt Margo Newman."

Pat interrupts, "What did you say?"

"Margo Newman's my aunt. She lives over in Modest Town near the Baptist church."

"She's my aunt, too! What's your name?"

"I'm Lou"

"You're my brother."

Wanda: "Oh isn't this just the picture of an ideal American family. Mom you never told me that you had a brother. So you're the idiot that came out of Aunt Margie's shack tonight."

"I wouldn't call myself an idiot. And what were you doing there?"

"It's none of your business."

Francie: "Why don't we sit in the waiting area? I'll lock the front door so that no clients come in and we can discuss this situation."

"There's nothing to discuss, Bitch."

"Wanda, what exactly is your problem? You don't show up for five days and you must think that I can do everything that needs to be completed by myself. It's irresponsible of you and I'm not going to tolerate this abuse any longer!"

"You know. I'm fed up with all of you. And now this low life uncle appears out of thin air. I don't think so."

Wanda takes from her Hoodie pocket her beloved Glock. She points it at Lou. Pat starts

186

screaming at Wanda.   Francie and Gertrude crouch behind a magazine rack. Sergeant and Bella stand in front of it.   Jodi and Ben enter the reception area from the kitchen.

"Wanda, put your gun down."

Wanda points her gun at Lou, and fires one shot. He goes down.

Ben and Jodi fire their weapons each hitting Wanda in both of her legs.   She goes down. Pat's screaming still holding the shaking Chihuahua.

There's pandemonium in this small waiting room as Lou and Wanda are bleeding and Pat doesn't know who to comfort.   Jodi and Ben apply pressure to wounds and a call is made to 9-1-1. Pat is hysterical and Mom looks like she's in a daze.   The drama that has gone down is too much.   Sergeant and Bella howl in unison as Pat screams.   The Chihuahua in her arms is howling, too.   Wanda's coherent enough to stick her middle finger up and her tongue out at me.

The ambulances arrive and cart Lou and Wanda off.   Since this is a crime scene, the agency is sealed.   I place a sign on the front door directing folks to travel to the main office in Accomack County.

About one hour or so later, Mom and I are sitting on the couch in my apartment having a glass of wine. Sophie, Sergeant and Bella are spread across my double bed.

There's a knock at the door and it's Jodi. She's all smiles. Chief Winston has told her that she can go on vacation. He feels as though the case has been solved and Jodi isn't needed. I'm all smiles, too, as I get to go to Key West.

Jodi: "I didn't have a chance to tell you this, but Sally-Sue is spending the night in jail."

"What!"

"There was a road block in front of Wallops and she was stopped. While the deputy was asking for Sally-Sue's license and county registration the officer's dog found pot in Sally-Sue's Biscotti jar. She denies that it's hers."

I smile and excuse myself to use the bathroom. I stand in front of the bathroom mirror and start some gyrations. I'm gyrating to the Rolling Stones song *You Can't Always Get What You Want*. I hear the words stinging my ears, *you can't always get what you want, you can't always get what you want, you can't always get what you want, but if you try sometimes, you just might find you get what you need.*

One more hip roll to the right and the word "Yes!" is screamed from my mouth, as I open the bathroom door and return to the living room with a smile on my face. Mom's smiling too; she knows how ugly Sally-Sue has been to me.

"What goes around comes around" as the saying goes.

Jodi: "The captain has given the letter that Gertrude found in Wanda's desk drawer to the Board of Social Services and a meeting has been called to discuss unethical hiring practices by Juney Bea Karring and Sally-Sue Moon. Both have been placed on administrative leave without pay pending investigation.

"Jodi, this is wonderful news. What time is our flight out of Norfolk?"

"We leave tomorrow afternoon."

"Mom, are you sure that you can stay for the week."

"Yes, Lonnie said that he would continue to care for my horses so it won't be a problem. In fact, I'm looking at this time in Chincoteague as a vacation. I can't wait to read a few books, drink wine and relax. I might even attend Sally-Sue's hearing.

"Mom, I forgot to show you something. Jodi knows." I get my cell phone from my pocket and press the video. I give mom the phone and her mouth drops about ten feet.

"Francie, is this Sally-Sue in purple thong underwear?"

"Yup. She fell out of the county car while getting gas. I told her that the gas tank was on the right side of the car, and she tried a short cut. I plan to put this on YouTube, but need to find

189

somebody to do it for me, as I don't want to lose my job."

Jodi: "I don't think that you would lose your job. I think that Sally-Sue's career is over. She was caught with pot in her possession while using a county vehicle. She may be pulling some time at the women's prison in Goochland."

It's about midnight when we have our last glass of wine. It's been a long five days. I still have a few things to pack prior to leaving tomorrow.

"What time are you picking me up, Jodi?"

"About one, we have an early evening flight."

18

Saturday arrived as I drank my last glass of wine. The morning brings sunshine and an early morning swipe to the face. Sophie wants me up as she desires tuna for breakfast. The moment that I stir Sergeant and Bella jump off of the bed and want to go outside.

Mom's in the kitchen making coffee and is frying omelets. There are biscuits in the oven. The apartment smells wonderful. I open a can of cat tuna and feed Sophie. Sergeant, Bella and I head for the stairs. It doesn't bother me a bit if I'm wearing my long pink robe. Who cares? I don't have a need to *dress for success* walking dogs.

Once breakfast is over, I head for the barn to ride Trooper. Mom and the dogs come too, piling into the Honda. It's cramped but what the heck. Watts Estates isn't that far from Chincoteague.

When we pull up to Elizabeth's farm, she's at the barn mucking horse stalls. Trooper's out in the pasture and has a new pasture mate, Woodrow. They look as though they like each other as no one is kicking or pinning ears.

"Hi, Elizabeth. How are you?"

"I heard that James was arrested."

"Yes he was, last night."

My dogs and Elizabeth's dog, Princess, are running circles around us. "Have you ever met my mom?"

"No."

"Well, this is my mom, Gertrude, and she's going to be taking care of my family while I'm in Key West for the week. I'm going with Investigator Burgess as her college friend contracted H1N1 and can't go. I'm really excited and need to get out of here. This has been a really stressful week."

"I know. James and I broke up. I'm seeing Bart."

Bart comes across his pasture to Elizabeth's barn. Introductions are made. I decide to go get Trooper from the pasture. He's in need of a good grooming and workout. Mom loves to ride so she can ride him during the week. This will be good for him to have somebody else on his back.

Elizabeth: "Bart, did you know that Investigator Burgess and Francie are headed for the Florida Keys?"

"I vacation in the Keys all the time. Where are you staying?"

"We're staying at Coconut Beach Resort; it's right on the Atlantic. Nice view of the ocean.

Rest and relaxation is just what the doctor ordered. I can't wait to get out of here.

I've got to go get Trooper as I need to be ready to go by one, when Jodi picks me up."

I watch Bart place his arms on Elizabeth's shoulders and I see that she stiffens under his touch. I'm wondering what's going on between them.

Trooper gives a good nicker when he sees me and I lead him out of the pasture. I groom him, giving him plenty of sugar cubes as the dogs run past me, around me and out into the pastures. Bart and Elizabeth are facing each other. Mom's reading a book, sitting on a lounge chair.

I tack Trooper and decide to work him in the pasture. He hasn't been ridden in a week and is full of energy. He puts his head down and gives three good bucks. I laugh and kick him into a canter and we're off. The cool air feels great on my face and I can feel my body relaxing. It has been such a tense week. This ride is really going to get me to loosen up for my vacation.

I can't help but think of Sally-Sue in jail on a pot charge. It serves her right for lying and being greedy. I ride for about thirty minutes and then decide to walk Trooper on a path leading to Chincoteague Channel. It's a beautiful day and Trooper's prancing. He wants to gallop along the water. I relax and let him go. He loves it.

193

Freedom and a gallop will do us good.   He settles down into a controlled canter and we gracefully move along with wind and water. What a natural high. It's great. I feel exuberant and Trooper feels spirited.

I walk Trooper back to the barn and cool him. He loves carrots and sugar cubes so I give him a few of each.   Mom pats him and we walk Trooper to his pasture.   Woodrow, a quarter horse, nays and is happy to be reunited with his pasture buddy.

Prior to leaving, I say good-bye to Elizabeth. She looks upset but doesn't want to talk about it. Oh well, when she wants to talk, I'll be there.

The dogs pile into the back of the Honda and mom and I return to my apartment.   I pack quickly, eat some yogurt and Jodi arrives. I grab my suitcase, kiss Mom goodbye and kiss each pet family member. Bella looks sad. Oh well, once I leave Mom will take good care of them.

I run down the steps and skip out the front door. Jodi is eagerly waiting for me with the trunk of her car open. She grabs my one bag and we're off. Too bad I don't have a joint. It would be so nice to have a smoke.

"We did it girlfriend! I can't believe that I'm getting to go on vacation."

"Me, too. What a week!"

We make good time, driving through Eastern Shore communities and come to the Chesapeake

194

Bay Bridge Tunnel. This bridge connects the Eastern Shore to the mainland of Virginia at Virginia Beach. It's miles of Atlantic Ocean and Chesapeake Bay and costs twelve bucks to go one way.

"Look at all the sea gulls sitting on the lamp posts, Jodi. Have you ever noticed how they face the same way? Have you noticed how many gulls are squished on the bridge?"

"I know. How can somebody hit a sea gull?"

"Gross."

We arrive at Norfolk International Airport and the flight's on time. We need to make a connection in Atlanta. The plane takes off and it's a beautiful November day. Trees still have a few colorful leaves. A few minutes after takeoff, there's an announcement by the pilot requesting a doctor.

Francie: "You can't be serious? Now what?"

"I don't know."

Two women stand up and speak with the stewardess. A pregnant woman is ushered to the back of the plane. Jodi and I are sitting midway by the wings and turn around and look.

"You can't tell me that this lady's going to have a baby on the plane, Jodi."

"I think she is girlfriend. We need to go with the flow. There's nothing anybody can do except deliver this baby."

195

In about ten minutes, with a cheering squad of two doctors and two stewardesses, and a hard long push, a squalling baby is delivered.

"Attention passengers, we have a new addition to this flight; a baby girl has just been delivered by two doctors and two of our crew. We're going to land briefly in Richmond so that mother and baby can get off of the plane and receive some medical attention."

Within minutes, we arrive at Richmond International Airport. We land and once in the air heading again for Atlanta, the stewardess announces that those with connections will be given first priority to leave the plane quickly upon landing.

We arrive in Atlanta and once off of the flight realize that we've missed our connection. Air Tran Airways is very accommodating and we are booked for the next flight out to Miami.

We arrive in Miami. The weather is about eighty with a slight breeze from the east. Everybody's speaking Spanish. I feel as though I'm in a foreign country.

Jodi: "I have rented an economy car from Thrifty."

"OK, let's go."

Key West, Florida, the most southern portion of the United States, is balmy and bright. The bridges going over to the Keys are low and near the crystal blue water. Jodi and I have smiles on our faces and our adrenaline is pumping. .

"Jodi, I'm so psyched!   This is wonderful. Thanks for inviting me."

Jodi looks at her left hand on the steering wheel and her yellow diamond is glistening.

"If we have time I would love to visit Hemingway's Estate as I want to see some of those famous cats with the extra toes."

"I want to take a day trip to Dry Tortugas National Park."

"What's that place all about, Jodi?"

"It's about seventy miles away on an island. There are wild birds and tales about pirates, and of course, somehow crocodiles have gotten there."

We arrive at Coconut Beach Resort at about eight and eagerly carry our bags into the tastefully decorated lobby.   Our room is absolutely gorgeous with two queen size beds, white wicker furniture, and tasteful artwork, with a sliding door opening to a balcony overlooking the Atlantic.

"Jodi, I can't thank you enough for inviting me.   I would never have gotten here on my own."

"Thanks for coming. Do you feel like going for a swim?"

"Of course. Let's put on our bathing suits."

We get on the elevator and I feel as though I'm living on a tropical island as the palm trees and bright colored flowering plants make perfect paths leading to the pools. Everything is at our fingertips. We jump into the deep end of the pool and the water is perfect. Not cold, but warm on our shoulders.

"I'm in heaven, Jodi."

"I know, partner in crime, just how you're feeling."

We swim a little, relax on lounge chairs and drink a few tropical drinks. I'm getting a good buzz. We watch the moon and stars for a bit and return to our room. We take naps, showers, and are energized for the night scene.

Jodi and I review a tourist book left in the room and decide on Sloppy Joe's, a popular historic bar and restaurant, which has been around since about 1933. It survived prohibition and Ernest Hemingway frequented the place. We leave the hotel and drive over.

"Neat place," I say as Jodi parks the car.

Upon entering we are mesmerized by the Cuban tiles, ceiling fans and jalousie doors. A huge stage and dance area is facing DuVal Street. The place is packed. Jodi and I find a spot, order drinks and begin to mingle and dance. By four, we're tired and decide to call it a day.

19

Gertrude's enjoying the crisp autumn day. She ties the dogs in the garden of Egret Moon Artworks so that she can enjoy shopping in her daughter's favorite store. Gertrude looks outside every few minutes to make sure that the pups are behaving. They're sitting, enjoying the day.
She purchases a pair of beaded earrings with matching bracelet, walks outside and sits in the lovely garden with the dogs smelling the fragrances of the last roses of summer.

After about a half hour, she gathers Sergeant and Bella and walks home. The dogs have enjoyed their outing. It's about three and Gertrude wants to check on Trooper. She puts the dogs in the back of the SUV and heads for Watts Estates.

Elizabeth and Bart are in the front of the barn. Princess is playing with the barn cat and spots Sergeant and Bella as they get out of the vehicle. The dogs play tag as Gertrude joins Elizabeth and Bart.

"Hi! How are you doing?"
Elizabeth: "OK. Are you planning to ride Trooper?"

"No. I just decided to come by and check on him. I might spend a few minutes grooming him."

Bart: "We've heard some rumors as to what happened over at social services late yesterday. Care to shed some light on the facts, since I've heard that you were there?"

"Actually, it was pretty intense. Wanda, an eligibility worker went off and shot her uncle in the leg. Ben Benson with the State Police and Investigator Burgess, shot Wanda in her legs. It looks like the Glock that she had is one that was used to murder all those people and Star or execute the Chincoteague pony."

Elizabeth: "Well, maybe life will settle. I can't imagine James doing anything this horrible. We have known each other since childhood. I know that he has moods, however, nothing this horrendous. I think that I'm going to visit him in the jail tomorrow. I called and found out visiting hours."

Bart: "I thought that you were through with the bastard."

Bart's outburst has taken Gertrude by surprise. Elizabeth replied by shrugging her shoulders and moving away from him.

"Well, ladies, I'm going. I have some plans for the evening."

Gertrude and Elizabeth watch Bart walk across the pasture to his house.

200

"Elizabeth, are you going out with Bart?"

"Sort-of. I feel that he's taking over my life though. Maybe James was right. What do I actually know about him?"

Bart's fed up. He's not having his needs met by Elizabeth. He gets into his truck and decides to drive around. He stops at a 7-11 and buys a beer and a lottery ticket, Mega Millions. He drives by Wallops and laughs at the insanity of James getting picked up. He's heard about Francie's supervisor, Sally-Sue Moon getting arrested for possession of pot.

He drives through Horntown. There's nothing much there and he continues to Horntown Landing. Bart gets out of his truck and takes in a view of the Chincoteague Bay and the Island of Chincoteague. He drinks his Pabst Blue Ribbon, a popular beer in Richmond, where he acquired a taste for the sweet brew during a card game that went sour in the capital city. Bart decides to get going and drives about two more miles to Sinnickson and gets out of the truck again. He walks down a path to The Old Tree. It's the largest tree that Bart's ever seen. Folks have been carving their names in the trunk for probably centuries. He stands admiring the tree and decides to go to 7-11 and get another Pabst Blue Ribbon.

It's Sunday morning about eleven and Chief Winston's enjoying the day with Ginger, his wife, when his pager goes off.

"Shit, what could it be now? Six months left before I can retire and it won't be soon enough."

He calls dispatch.

"There's been another killing."

"You can't be serious. I thought that we caught the mothers. I will be right in."

"Ginger, I need to take you home, honey. Something's happened. There's been another killing. We obviously didn't catch the right asshole."

Ben Benson's on his way to Northern Virginia when his cell phone rings.

"Ben this is Chief Winston. Where are you? We've had another murder."

"What?"

"You need to come back to Chincoteague immediately. We've arrested the wrong killers."

"OK. I'm on my way."

With that, Ben makes a U-turn, shoves his left hand out the driver side window placing flashing blue lights onto the car roof and floors the car south.

Investigator Andy Walsh's pager and cell phone go off simultaneously. There's a mandatory meeting at twelve.

Elizabeth Allen has finished mucking stalls and goes out to the pasture to check on Trooper and Woodrow.   Somebody has put a halter on Trooper. She climbs the wooden horse fence and walks midway as Trooper sees Elizabeth and comes to greet her. The red nylon halter, doesn't fit as it's too tight. On the side of the halter there's a note attached.   Elizabeth turns Trooper's face and reads the note: "You're next Bitch." Elizabeth runs out of the pasture directly to Bart's house. She knocks on the back door. He doesn't answer. She uses her cell phone to call 9-1-1.

 At twelve all deputies and the same state troopers reunite in the conference room of the precinct. Investigator Jodi Burgess is the only member missing. Chief Winston is beyond the point of anger. No words can describe how irate he is. This murderer is making a fool out of him and his department.

"I've called us together as there's been another murder. This time in Sinnickson at The Old Tree. One female and one male found sitting under it, shot in their foreheads. They were positioned holding a horse wind chime. I need two volunteers to go out to Helltown and stake out Margo Newman's house.

Investigator Andy Walsh and Deputy Doreen Martin raise their hands.

"I want you to stake out the place and count how many horse wind chimes are left on the tree and how many have been taken. You should see about 7 chains hanging without chimes. My theory is that the killer returned to Margo Newman's and took another chime. I want you to interview the old lady. I understand that she's demented, but try to get some information from her. I want this place staked out 24-7. Call in when you want to be relieved from duty."

Ben Benson: "We don't have the ballistic report yet on the two Glocks. Until we receive information, Wanda Burton and James Parker will remain in jail. We either have arrested the right individuals or have a copycat killer on the loose, or we jailed the wrong folks. Remember, two Glocks have been used. One to kill the Chincoteague pony and the other was used on Tony Smith, Maureen Hughes, Michael Surry, Sally and Ned Melton and Star, the horse. The ballistic report is top priority and we should have results within the hour."

Chief Winston: "I have just been informed that Elizabeth Allen has called emergency. She's the woman whose friend's horse, Star, was murdered. Evidently she walked out to one of her pastures and a note was attached to a horse named Trooper owned by Francie Batista. Francie's on vacation with Investigator Burgess.

I will be contacting Jodi as soon as this meeting ends."

I'm having brunch at poolside with Jodi when her cell phone goes off. She looks at the number and realizes that it's an emergency from dispatch.

"Francie, I'm going to go back to our room to answer the call. It appears that it's work related and an emergency. It's probably Millie, our secretary, needing to have a question answered about the police report that I completed on James Parker, Sally-Sue Moon or Wanda Burton. I was in a hurry when I finished the paperwork."

"OK." I get up from the table and point to a place with two lounge chairs next to the pool. "I'll just sunbathe and swim until you get back."

Jodi leaves and I get comfortable on the lounge chair. I place it in the recliner position and begin to soak in the rays. What a beautiful Saturday. The vegetation and flowering tropical plants are brilliant in colors. I close my eyes and nod off for about fifteen minutes. I'm awakened by the sense that someone's watching me. I open my eyes and look to the right lounge chair thinking that Jodi has returned.

"My God, you've scared the hell out of me, Bart. What are you doing here?"

"I have a friend living here so I thought I'd visit for a week or so. Where's Jodi?"

205

"Her cell phone went off and it was work related so she went back to our room to call dispatch. She thinks that there's some glitch with the paperwork that she completed in a rush."

"I have an idea. I'm staying with a friend about five blocks from here. Why don't you come with me and we can hang together for the day? We'll give Jodi a call with directions and she can come over once she's off of the phone. You know her cell number, don't you?"

"I don't know, Bart. We were going to plan to hang out together. She might get mad at me if I take off with you."

"Francie, you're not taking off with me. Jodi can join us and then you two can leave and do your thing. My friend's place is really nice and I'd like for you to meet him. You and he may hit it off, you never know. It will be fun."

"OK. I'll go. I'll give Jodi a call in about twenty minutes. She won't believe that you're here!" I gather my beach bag, cell and sunscreen and follow Bart to the parking lot.

20

Jodi returns to her room and calls dispatch. Immediately, Brittany picks up the phone.

"Jodi, hold on, Ben Benson and the Chief want to talk to you."

"Oh, what's the problem Brittany?"

"You need to speak with them. Here they are coming back to the captain's office. I'm transferring the call, please hold, Jodi."

"Hello, Jodi, we've got a mess up here."

"What's the problem, Chief Winston?"

"We've had another execution, a man and a woman found under The Old Tree in Sinnickson. They were discovered early this morning holding a horse wind chime by some tourist who wanted to see this famous tree. It's just like the other murders. Also, dispatch just got a call from Elizabeth Allen. There was a hand written note attached to Francie Batista's horse's halter. It said, "You're next Bitch.""

"When I tell Francie about Trooper and this note she's really going to be upset. Is the horse alright?"

Ben Benson: "I haven't heard otherwise. I'm concerned about her safety. Did she inform a lot of friends that she was going to the Keys?"

"She told co-workers and of course Elizabeth, who's taking care of her horse.   Gertrude, Francie's mother is staying at her daughter's apartment caring for Francie's pets."

"Well, I'll place an officer outside of her apartment, just to make sure that Gertrude isn't targeted. I think that the killer is after Francie."

"Francie has said this more than once to me. I just thought that she was overreacting to events. I'll keep close tabs on her and if there's a problem, I'll contact you. Thanks for the info."

Ben Benson: "Oh and I almost forgot, about ten minutes ago we received the ballistics report on the two Glocks. The Glock owned by Wanda Burton didn't kill the pony, horse or people. James Parker's Glock killed the pony."

"You're right, what a mess. I wonder who's operating the third Glock?"
Jodi hangs up and quickly leaves the room to return to poolside.

Francie's impressed at the BMW M3 Convertible that Bart's leased. It's dark blue and has some sparkle to it. Jodi would like it for its bling.

"Nice touch Bart. I like."

"It rides like a dream."

We head away from the Coconut Beach Resort and drive alongside of the ocean traveling to the center of Old Town Key West. The mansions are incredibly beautiful in this area of the Keys. We pull into the driveway of a house on Elizabeth Street. Up goes the garage door and Bart pulls his BMW into the garage. We walk in through the garage to the kitchen and great room area. For me, my little apartment would fit inside of this garage. I spot the pool and want to check it out.

"Bart, I think that it's been about twenty minutes. I need to call Jodi and give her the address to this magnificent place."

Bart walks over and stands in front of me. He's in my space making me feel uncomfortable. I ignore him and bend down to reach my beach bag in order to obtain my cell phone.

"By the way, where's your friend?" I look down to speed dial Jodi and the next thing I know Bart has me in a choke hold. My air is being cut off. I feel faint and my cell phone hits the floor and the battery glides across the gray tiled floor.

In college I took a one credit course in personal defense, so I elbow him in his right ribs, and simultaneously kick my leg back and nail him between the legs, directly in the bastard's crotch. He's off balance and holding onto the family jewels as I start to run.

I don't know the layout of the house so I run outside to the pool area. I'm screaming, "fire; call 9-1-1" and trampling the carefully manicured gardens. A high privacy fence outlines the yard. I look behind me and see Bart coming out onto the patio. He has a gun in his right hand and a wind chime in his left. *Oh my God, he's the killer. Jesus, Mary and Joseph have mercy on me. Now I lay me down to sleep...*

Jodi comes to poolside, doesn't see Francie and is alarmed. No Francie. She's gone. Her stuff's gone.

Jodi sees a security guard. "I left my girlfriend a few minutes ago to return to my room. Have you seen a young girl with short curly hair, about twenty, sitting by the pool?"

"She left with a young guy in his mid-twenties about thirty minutes ago."

Jodi goes into her beach bag and shows her police badge to the security guard.

"Call the police. I think that my friend has just been kidnapped by the Chincoteague wind chime killer."

Jodi dials Chief Winston.

"Francie's missing. I think that the killer has followed us down here. I've just asked the security guard to call the police. Do you have any more information?"

210

"Two more wind chimes are missing from Margo Newman's tree.   I sent a deputy to Elizabeth Allen's farm to interview her and to obtain the note left on Trooper's halter.   The State Police profiler, Trooper Goode, is going to look at it."

"OK. I'll get back with you."

Two Key West deputies arrive at the resort. They are introduced to Jodi by the security guard, Neil Akers.   Jodi is beside herself with concern. She shows her identification and briefs Deputy Myers and Deputy Tony about the events on the Eastern Shore.   Neil Akers gives a description of the man who escorted Francie from the pool to the parking area. The young man was driving a dark blue BMW M3 Convertible.   Deputy Myers calls dispatch and requests names of individuals who have leased this type of vehicle in the Miami and Key West area.

I run towards the back of the yard and see a shed. Nobody's around to hear me screaming and I decide to stop yelling, as I don't want Bart to find me in this jungle of a back yard. There's a brown and white shed near the back privacy fence. I run up to it and it's unlocked. I'm hesitant to go inside as there's no back door to escape. *I'll be like a caged animal if Bart comes through the door and knows that I'm hiding in*

211

here. When I took that lousy one credit personal defense course, the instructress never talked about what to do if one is in this type of situation.

I rush in and climb over a bunch of yard furniture and pool equipment. I stumble and see a hatchet on the floor. I pick it up and decide that I may need to use this as a weapon, although Bart's got a gun. I climb to the back right corner of the shed holding my hatchet for dear life. I pray to St. Anthony. This is definitely the time to pray to him. I'm in need of a miracle for this hopeless situation that I've gotten myself in.

I place some furniture and pool equipment in front of me and hide, so I'm able to see the door, if it opens. I should have been a better Catholic, learned my religion and listened to the nuns. If I get out of this ghastly situation I'm going to confession. I haven't gone since I made my First Holy Communion. Maybe a career helping others will help give me some eminence with God?

Deputies Myers and Tony start alerts and soon Francie's photo is all over Breaking News. Luckily, Jodi had a picture of Francie taken with Sergeant and Bella last week on her cell.

Within one hour, Deputy Tony obtains the information about a rented BMW from Miami leased early this morning.   The car has been leased by Bart Connors.

Jodi calls Chief Winston. "The BMW that the security guard saw Francie getting into was leased by Bart Connors."

"Watch your back Jodi. Good work. I'll have Ben Benson and one of my deputies go over to his farm. I'll call you if we find anything of importance."

Bart's walking all over the yard looking for Francie. It's a tropical forest and difficult to see every inch. *I've got to hand it to the Bitch; she gave me a good elbow in the ribs and a swift well-placed kick. She'll pay for that.*
Bart looks under the cover of the hot tub and stares into the pool to see if she's holding her breath under the water. It has been about two hours since Francie and he left the resort. *I bet Jodi has everybody and their mother looking for her. I thought that this was going to be easy to do.*

Bart comes to a shed and smiles. He opens the door.

There's been a 9-1-1 call received regarding a fire on Elizabeth Street. Fire and Rescue are on the way. Jodi feels certain that Francie is behind this as when Francie's apartment was broken into last week she screamed "fire."

213

"I think that this call is about Francie as she screamed "fire" a week ago when somebody tried to get into her apartment. Let's go."

The deputies put in a call for back up and drive with sirens wailing to the Elizabeth Street house. When they arrive, Deputy Myers and Tony draw their weapons.   Jodi feels naked without hers and, therefore, lingers behind them. They look in the window of the garage and see the BMW. Deputy Myers eyes his partner to move forward.   They edge toward the side entrance.
Jodi stays back as the SWAT team has arrived and has assembled. Some officers go to the front of the house and others to the back.

Bart walks inside of the shed. I can see him holding his gun and pointing it. *I promise God that if I make it out of this alive that I will go to church every Sunday and Holy Days.* My heart is racing. I can see my shirt moving. *I need to hold my breath so that he can't hear me breathing.*

"Come out, Bitch. I know that you're in here." Bart picks up a folded chair and flings it onto the back wall barely missing Francie's head. He makes his way slowly over pool equipment, making sure that he keeps his balance.

214

Deputies Myers and Tony continue edging their way through the backyard. Tropical trees are blocking their vision and they're tense. They see the pool and hot tub and continue forward, eyeing the back portion of the yard.   In the distance Deputy Tony spots a small shed. He motions for his partner, directing his eyes to the shed.

I sensed that Bart saw me crouched and hiding. I couldn't continue to hold my breath any longer. I heard his breathing and it was deep and labored. I waited for Bart to take one more step. I held onto my hatchet with all of my might, screamed and swung the hatchet like a baseball bat as he pointed the gun. I hit the bastard in his abdomen as his gun went off and hit me in my right shoulder.

Jodi's by the pool and hears Francie scream. She has partnered with another deputy.   Deputies Myers and Tony come to the front of the shed. They have heard a gun fire.

"Bart Connors, we have the place surrounded. Come out with your hands up by the count of three or we're coming in. 1-2-3." No Bart.

Deputy Myers walks inside the shed and sees Bart holding his abdomen with the gun dangling from his right hand. Blood is pulsating out from his abdomen.

215

Bart turns and fires at Deputy Myers. Deputy Myers exchanges fire hitting Bart in his chest. He staggers and falls onto a lawn mower, dying instantly. A wind chime clangs and gets tangled in his left hand as he hits the lawn mower.

Jodi's made her way swiftly to the shed. She has heard the gun fire and fears the worst.

"Francie, are you in there?"

I'm still in a crouched position. I've been hit in the shoulder. I stand up holding my bloody hatchet in my right hand and with my left hand; attempt to cover my wound.

Two deputies come in and help me out of this cluttered shed. I walk over Bart to get out of the shed trying not to look.

I see Jodi. She's crying.

"I'm so sorry that I didn't wait for you to come back to the pool. I hope that you're not mad at me, Jodi. Bart said that we would call you in twenty minutes."

"It's OK. Let's get you in the ambulance and get this shoulder looked at, girlfriend."

"Jodi, I'm just so sorry."

I'm rushed to Fisherman's Hospital. Jodi comes with me in the ambulance. I'm examined in the emergency room. The bullet grazed my shoulder. I'm given a Tetanus shot, stitches, and a prescription for pain and released. Jodi calls a cab and we return to Coconut Beach Resort.

Chief Winston's sitting at his desk and receives a call from Jodi.

"Bart's dead. He had Francie trapped in a shed. We got there just in time. Florida State Police will send you a report. Bart's the wind chime killer as he had a Glock and was holding a wind chime when he went down."

"How's Francie? She's in bed as a bullet grazed her right shoulder. The doctor gave the wound a few stitches, and she is taking pain pills. Francie's resting now. Do you have any information on Bart Connors?"

"I'll explain when you return on Saturday. Enjoy the rest of your time off."

"Yeah, sure. Thanks."

The remainder of our week is a blur. Pain, along with anxiety, gripped me. Jodi took good care of me, never leaving my side. We sunbathed by the pool for the rest of the week. I think that I slept most of the time. Jodi called it shock. One unanswered question: Why would Bart Connors want to kill me?

Mom absolutely lost it when Jodi called her while I was asleep that first night. Jodi had wanted to be the first to speak with mom as she

217

feared the grape vine effect and didn't want mom to hear it from others.

Mom, in turn, called Elizabeth Allen who upon hearing that the killer was Bart called her doctor and had her tranquilizer prescription renewed. Obviously, she absolutely freaked that the two men in her life had committed murder.

We returned to the Eastern Shore and to Chincoteague late Saturday night. One week away from the island and so much happened. My mind kept repeating events every day. I walked around numb, obsessed.

On Sunday morning, Mom and I went to Mass at St. Andrew's, a Catholic church located on Church Street. It's a charming friendly church with everybody smiling and happy. Maybe I'll join the choir as I plan to be attending church for a long time. Like my whole life. St. Anthony, the saint of hopeless causes saved me.

21

It's Monday and I still don't trust that day. The alarm's just gone off and Sergeant and Bella want to go outside and of course, Sophie wants her tuna.

Nobody gives me a moment to wake up or permit me to just lie in bed. I'm still tired, even though I've slept a good eight hours.

As I stretch, I grab my pink robe, place my feet into my worn slippers, open a can of tuna for my cat and out the door I go with the dogs. Tails wagging, they charge down the steps to the yard.

It has been six months since I almost met my demise. There have been a lot of changes around social services as I have a new supervisor these days. Paul Housemen was hired about four months ago. The Board of Social Services got smart and hired a man. No performing, no nepotism, no queen for the day and no purple thong underwear. Well, I hope not, although one never knows until your co-worker falls out of a county car.

I really don't know where to start so I'll start with Sally-Sue Moon. Sally-Sue isn't going to complete her thirty years working as a social worker. She was fired having been found guilty by the court for possession of marijuana.

I sat with Mom and Jodi during the court hearing trying not to smirk. Sally-Sue was lead into the courtroom and lead out of the courtroom pleading that she was innocent, a victim. On the day of court she wore a purple linen pantsuit and thong sandals. Her perfume was, you guessed it, Patchouli Oil.

Juney Bea served as a character witness for her friend and of course, that didn't go over well as Juney Bea was in trouble, too.

As the verdict was rendered and read out loud, Sally-Sue's final words as she was handcuffed and lead out of the courtroom was that the pot had to have been Wanda's.

"Somebody's got to believe me, it wasn't my pot."

I did squirm a little, maybe even had an ounce of Italian guilt, however; the thought and feelings quickly dissipated.

Juney Bea Karring was fired as Director. The Board of Social Services unanimously voted that there was enough evidence to support her tainted hiring practices.

The note card found by my mom, written by Wanda's mother, Pat, as well as an interview with Wanda's mother, determined without doubt

220

that Wanda did not have credentials to be hired as an eligibility worker.

I last heard that Juney Bea is employed by Bargain Basement of New York and is a buyer for the store.   She sorts through garbage of the rich and famous living in apartments near Central Park.   I've been told that she was recently seen in the background of the Today Show with a shopping cart full of clothing, and holding a sign, "Dress for Success."

Pat relocated to the Eastern Shore to live with her brother, Lou Mann. They decided to take care of Aunt Margo. The "salt box" house became presentable. Lou climbed the oak tree and got rid of all of the wind chimes.   Aunt Margo, the hound dog and Chihuahua named Diva, are well taken care of.

I got to close Margo Newman's case as she's no longer at risk. Good for me, as I have one less client to be concerned about. This definitely had a happy ending.

Lou is feeling lucky these days.   He isn't homeless and has found his sister.   Lou's followed by the local mental health clinic and is taking medication for his schizophrenia. The voices come less often and don't bother him.

Jodi received a promotion. She's Sergeant Jodi Burgess and no longer lives in Chincoteague.

Jodi's working in Norfolk in charge of the Cold Case Unit. We speak daily. "Girlfriends" and as she says, "Partners in crime" followed by her sweet giggle.

She visits Chincoteague monthly and we spend time eating doughnuts and visiting Jon and Jane at Sundial Books, enjoying coffee, atmosphere and conversation.

Captain Winston's newly retired. Ben Benson and the Chief were recent guests of honor at the governor's mansion. The Eastern Shore wind chime killer, Bart Connors, was profiled on the show, *48 Hours*.

Captain Winston and Ben plan to co-author a book about what happened in this peaceful community. Of course, Captain Winston did retire in glory and Jodi and I attended his retirement party at Bill's Restaurant, his favorite hangout.

James Parker's serving two years for killing the Chincoteague pony and he's receiving substance abuse and anger control counseling.

Elizabeth's been visiting him in jail and they're engaged. He says that he's found God and is a changed person. I do believe that folks can find religion under stressful conditions and am hopeful that James has changed.

Wanda Burton was found not guilty of shooting her uncle, Lou Mann, by reason of insanity. She's currently receiving treatment at Central State Hospital. Wanda, according to Pat, is happy. Recently the therapist placed her in charge of a trap-neuter-release program of feral cats within the hospital grounds. Wanda's content to spend the rest of her life at Central State caring for cats.

There's not much to report about Bart Connors. He had a troubled youth, didn't like his parents and brother much and thought that he was going to find his pot of gold in Margo Newman's house. As a child, he remembered visiting his great aunt and listening to her talk about the legend of wind chimes. He was fascinated by this folklore according to his father, George.

Since I'm a social worker and interested in family relationships, I discovered that Bart's father, George was Pat and Lou's first cousin. George's father, Lewis, is their father Neil's brother and therefore their uncle. Pat and Lou had never been told that their father had a brother. Evidently, Lewis left the Eastern Shore after high school and did not communicate with family. Who knew?

Why Bart hated social workers is beyond me. It probably had something to do with his youth, as he was involved with therapists and school social workers. No one will ever know why he acted in this manner, but one thing's for sure, he didn't like me. I think he was afraid that I was going to solve the murders due to my background as a social worker. I was right that he killed the wrong horse at Elizabeth's farm.

And then there's me. I'm happy to be alive and like James became more religious. What's good is that I have permission from my new boss that I can bring my dogs to work with me. Sergeant and Bella love coming to the agency, meeting clients, who pet and make a fuss over them.
Sophie, my cat, enjoys time spent away from the dogs as she spends her days on my antique double bed, drifting off to sleep in the afternoon sun.

Mom returned to Charlottesville and calls every day. If I don't pick up and answer the cell phone she calls Jodi, who calls a deputy who comes to visit me and directs me to call Mom. This micromanaging does get on my nerves. I feel that I've lost freedom. Maybe in about one year life will settle for me.

I do have one piece of unfinished business though; I haven't attended confession. I don't know quite how to explain to Father Grimes that the marijuana in the Biscotti jar was mine.

WIND CHIMES   Teresa Adele Bettino

Oh well, for now it's Monday and it's not hot, foggy, buggy or rainy. It's just Monday and I have clients to visit.

Books by Teresa Adele Bettino

The Adventures of Sugarbabe and Thunder

The Ten Commandments of a Welfare Worker

Degen and Me

The Cats of Hanover Juvenile Correctional Center

Unique Shadows

A Wicker Rocker

Two Dogs and a Boy

About Fer-Sher Publishing

Fer-Sher Publishing was established in 2006 with the publication of *Primary Concerns* By Sherry Ferrell and several titles written by Miriam J. Walker. Teresa Adele Bettino's *A Wicker Rocker* was published in 2007, and *Two Dogs and A Boy* in 2008.

For more information visit our website at: *www.fersherpublishing.com*

Teresa Adele Bettino was born in East Orange New Jersey. A retired social worker, Teresa resides in Mechanicsville, Virginia.

Partial proceeds from book sales will be donated to animal rescue.

Photo:
Courtesy Nancy Wilmink